Crack! The whip snapped. Suddenly, the tiger leaped at the trainer.

The audience gasped. Women began to scream. Jimmy wanted to hold his hands over his ears, but instead he gripped the arm rests of his seat and wouldn't let go.

The tremendous strength of the tiger's paw caused Anna's father to reel back, stumble against a wooden block, and fall down. Anna didn't waste time screaming, but quickly took up her bull whip and gave it a powerful crack. The lash struck the cat across its back. The tiger roared and ran a few paces; then stopped and turned back, lips curled in a snarl. Anna's father pulled himself up, holding his side. The tiger flattened its ears and began to stalk the man. Stealthily, it moved closer, closer, closer. . . .

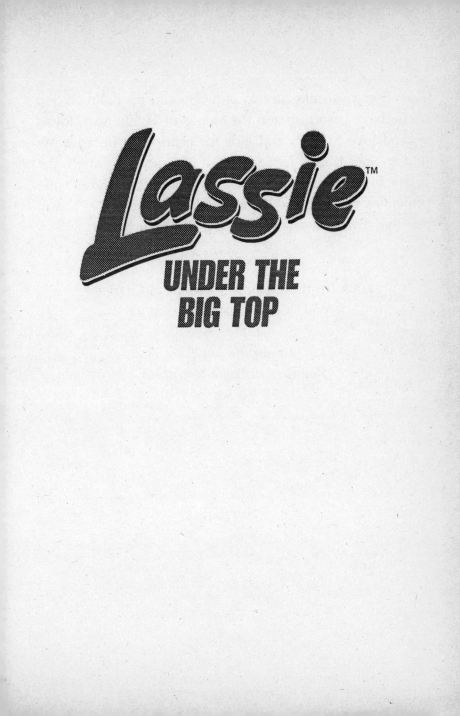

Lassie™

UNDER THE BIG TOP

These heartwarming stories of a boy and his beloved dog Lassie have demonstrated the values of faithfulness, loyalty, and love to boys and girls for nearly five decades. As Jimmy and Lassie face different situations through the Lassie stories from Chariot Family Publishing, these same principles will come alive for children of the 90s in a way that they can understand and apply to their lives.

Look for these Lassie books from Chariot
at your local Christian bookstore.

Under the Big Top
Treasure at Eagle Mountain
To the Rescue

Lassie™

UNDER THE BIG TOP

Adapted by
Marian Bray

Chariot Books™
*A Division of Cook
Communications Ministries*

Chariot Books™ is an imprint of Chariot Family Publishing
Cook Communications Ministries, Elgin, Illinois 60120
Cook Communications Ministries, Paris, Ontario
Kingsway Communications, Eastbourne, England

Cover illustration by Ron Mazellan
Cover design by Joe Ragont Studios

First Printing, 1995
Printed in United States of America
99 98 97 96 95   5 4 3 2 1

Under the Big Top is a Christian adaptation
of characters and situations based on the
Lassie television series. TV scripts are used by
permission of the copyright holder.

Table of Contents

A Furry Gift

Twelve-year-old Jimmy Harmon and his mom, Ruth Harmon, stepped out of Farley's Athletic Shoe Store into the spring afternoon sunlight. Jimmy bounced lightly on his toes, flexing his arches. In these new shoes, he could run forever.

"I'm gonna get Lassie and go, okay?" he asked his mom. The shopping center was two point four miles from home. He and Lassie could run it easily.

"Okay, I'll see you at home," Mom said as she took the car keys out of her purse.

At the same moment, Jimmy and Mrs. Harmon glanced toward the car and saw that the passenger side door was open. And Lassie, their tricolored, rough coat collie wasn't in her usual place in the backseat of the car.

"Oh, no, I forgot to lock the door," he said and leaped onto a bench beside Warren's Frozen Yogurt Shoppe. Jimmy cupped his hands and called, "Lassie," as he scanned the parking lot for his dog.

Mrs. Harmon stood shading her eyes, searching the lot crowded with the before dinner shopping rush. "It's not like her to get out and run off," she murmured to herself, but Jimmy heard her and knew she was right.

Jimmy called the collie's name again.

He and his dad had taught Lassie to open the car door after they'd seen a police dog demonstration. The hulking K-9 German shepherds had been taught to press the door handle and jump out to go to the aid of their handlers.

After a couple days of training, Lassie had learned the same trick. She would press the car door handle, push the door open with her head and hop out. Lassie was so good at it, in fact, that if they left her in the car more than a couple minutes they had to lock the doors or she'd skip out. She never strayed far, though. Usually she'd sprawl in a patch of sunlight or if it was raining or snowing, she'd creep under the car as if it was her den.

Once the family had left her in the car during an evening church service. They were going away on vacation after Dad preached. Once again, Jimmy had forgotten to lock his car door and about five minutes into Dad's sermon, Jimmy heard nails clicking on the wooden church aisle floor. Lassie strolled on down the main aisle of church, plunked herself down next to Jimmy, then gave a huge sigh as if to say, "Is that guy talking again?"

A door opening along the covered mall aisle caught

Jimmy's eye. A woman held the door for a slim-faced collie. His collie. Lassie.

"There she is," called Jimmy. He leaped down and ran up to her. Lassie wagged her feathery tail and barked at him, then at the woman, as if trying to introduce them.

"She was visiting the puppies," said the woman who patted Lassie's head. The shop was Little Critters Pet Store. Five fat bellied puppies crawled over each other in the window display. "I think the puppies were weaned too early. They've been crying a lot. Your dog came to see them so I let her in to get a better look. The puppies quieted right down. I'm glad you sent her over here."

Jimmy thanked the woman for watching Lassie. It was too complicated to explain that Lassie had opened the car door by herself and had gone visiting on her own.

As the pet store clerk went back inside, the sound of crying puppies came out. Lassie whined.

"Sorry, girl," said Jimmy. "We can't stay. We've got to jog home, remember?" Jimmy waved an all right sign to his mom and she shut the door Lassie had left open, got into the car, and drove off.

"Lassie, heel," commanded Jimmy and the collie slid beside him. Without a leash, Lassie heeled easily, her body level with Jimmy's knees. As she trotted beside him, her gold, onyx, and white fur rippled in the cool air.

They ran across the shopping center parking lot, onto

the sidewalk and headed north for home. They passed a tire store; the main library; and Jimmy's school, Farley Middle School, where he was in sixth grade. Next year he'd be able to join the cross country and track teams. He could hardly wait. He thought it was dumb that his school didn't have track teams for his grade.

Jimmy and Lassie crossed two more streets, pausing for one red light. Lassie sat automatically as he stopped. Then she heeled once more as he took off. Dad had helped him train her to heel, sit, drop, stay, and come. Last year Jimmy had entered her in a dog obedience show and they had taken second place! She probably would have been first if he hadn't goofed up and forgotten to make her walk around behind him to finish properly. Oh, well.

"Next fall," he promised her. "We'll enter again and you'll win first place."

She pricked her ears at the sound of his voice, her large eyes looking on his face.

Sometimes he loved her so much that it scared him.

If anything ever happened to her. . . .

Don't think that, he told himself. Besides, God will take care of her. God cared for even the sparrow, so he would certainly care for Lassie.

Jimmy and Lassie crossed another street. This was Center Street. One block to the west was the church where his dad was the pastor.

Lassie gave a low whine as if she knew Mr. Harmon was near.

"Yeah, I know," Jimmy said. "You want to go over to the church to see Dad, but we don't have time now."

Lassie loved all the Harmons—Dad, Mom, and even his obnoxious 10-year-old sister, Sarah. But everyone knew Lassie was *his* dog. And Jimmy was her person. Simple. No argument. But even though everyone knew that, they all loved her, especially Dad. He had had a dog when he was a kid so he knew exactly how Jimmy felt about Lassie.

Some people at church made snide remarks when his dad spoke so highly of Lassie. They thought of her as just another animal, like a dumb cow or sheep. Lassie was zillions of times more than that. She was like a brother, a friend, a companion, all rolled into one furry person.

Dad just told him not to worry about what others said. "They don't understand about Lassie. She is a gift from God."

And that she was, a gift wrapped in silky fur.

2

The Wire That Binds

A quarter of a mile from the house where Jimmy and his family lived, was another smaller shopping center. Among the shops was Madison's Hardware Store.

"Want to see Rags?" Jimmy asked Lassie as they approached the store. She looked around as if searching for her friend. Jimmy added, "Let's check if Rags is here."

He always acted like he stopped by Madison's Hardware so Lassie could play with Rags, but really he stopped because he hoped to see Katie Madison. She was different from the other girls he knew, especially his sister, Sarah. Sarah was strictly a nuisance in his book. Now, Katie, . . . she was fun.

Jimmy and Lassie jogged around the building to the back door of the hardware store. A small bay dipped down to an open freight door. A tool and hardware truck was backed up to the bay and a man unloaded boxes.

Jimmy slipped inside the open door, crossing in front of the small electric forklift and threaded around the piles of crates filled with nails, screws, hammers, axes, power tools, and every other interesting thing he could possibly imagine. Jimmy thought he wouldn't mind owning a hardware store one day.

Dan Madison, Katie's father, was talking to the truck driver who was wearing a long sleeved T-shirt that read: We Sell Only the Best. His arm muscles bulged through the blue shirt sleeves and Jimmy wondered if he'd even have one muscle that looked that good. He and Lassie were strong, but skinny.

"Tough and stringy," his mother would pronounce while squeezing his arm. Jimmy wasn't sure if that was really good, but he guessed it was the truth and you couldn't argue with the truth, now could you?

Mr. Madison noticed him and stopped talking to the truck driver. "Hey, Jim. What can I do for you today?"

"Is Rags here? And Katie?" He flushed because he'd asked for the dog first, instead of Katie. Mr. Madison would think he was such a dolt!

But Mr. Madison simply smiled and waved him to the main store. "Working in there with her granny."

As Jimmy and Lassie stepped by, Mr. Madison called, "Hey, girl," and petted Lassie.

The built guy commented, "Nice dog."

"She is," Mr. Madison said. "Jimmy's dog is well trained. Smart, too. I keep waiting for the day she starts talking."

Jimmy flushed again, this time with pride. He and Lassie darted into the store and found Katie sitting on the floor in the plumbing aisle, frowning at a clipboard in her lap. Her long reddish brown hair swept down her back. A pencil was tucked behind her ear.

Rags, her small, long haired, mop of a dog, sprang up with a joyous yip. Katie glanced up and her frown melted to a smile. She was easily the prettiest girl Jimmy had ever seen.

"Hi, Jimmy," she said.

"Hi," he responded as he sat down to join her.

Lassie crouched, her front legs straight, her rump and tail high, telling Rags in dog language, "Let's play!"

Rags yipped in agreement and they darted off down the plumbing aisle and vanished up the paint aisle.

"Oh, no," Katie laughed. "Gran's not going to like dogs running through the store." Katie's grandmother, Rachel Madison, owned Madison's Hardware Store.

Jimmy whistled for Lassie, but Lassie didn't listen or obey. She never did around Rags. They egged each other on, like two mischievous kids. They always got into trouble together.

In the garden section a woman shrieked.

Jimmy and Katie looked at each other. Katie dropped the clipboard, got up, and ran down the aisle. Jimmy followed close behind her.

"Lassie," Jimmy called again as Katie said, "Oh no, Rags!" The dogs weren't in the garden section any more. Jimmy heard barking so he darted down the power tool aisle with Katie fast after him. The two dogs streaked out of another aisle across their path.

"Outside, Lassie, outside," yelled Jimmy, hoping she'd head for the bay doors in the back where she often played with Rags.

"Rags, Rags!" called Katie. "Come here now."

The dogs headed in the opposite direction, to the front of the store.

Near the checkout lanes, a little kid hollered gleefully, "Doggie!"

Above the barking and shouting voices, a stern woman's voice rang out: "Kathryn!"

Katie rolled her eyes and mouthed, "Gran."

Jimmy and Katie stopped at the first checkout aisle. A silver haired woman in a sensible brown skirt and matching brown blouse stood, hands on ample hips. "Kathryn, does my hardware store look like a kennel?"

"No, Gran," Katie said respectfully.

Jimmy nearly laughed out loud, but pinched the inside of his elbow to stop the chuckles.

"Then get those dogs out of my store!"

"Yes, Gran," said Katie, just as respectfully, but Jimmy could tell she was holding back laughter. They shot after their dogs, who fortunately had sensed displeasure and darted to the back.

Mr. Madison and the truck driver were still talking and barely looked up as the two dogs, then the two kids, roared past.

Outside Jimmy and Katie gulped the cool afternoon air and laughed and laughed.

Lassie chased the little animated mop that was her buddy. Sometimes she wasn't sure if she was chasing the dog's head or tail. They looked the same. But whatever the case, the little dog moved fast.

Rags zigged and zagged across the back parking lot. After leading Lassie around in a crazy pattern, he darted under the parked truck and panted for breath.

Lassie whined, peering under the truck, unable to squeeze her bigger body after the little dog. No fair! she seemed to say.

So Rags shot out. He galloped up the ramp of the bay. Lassie streaked after him, her open, panting mouth nearly biting Rags' wiry tail. Suddenly Rags did a fast ninety degree turn and dove into the open truck bed.

Lassie trailed Rags into the truck. She was moving slower, unable to twist and turn as easily as the small dog who jetted around the towers of crates and pallets of stacked boxes. The inside of the truck was dim. It smelled sharp of burned brake pads and searing diesel fuel. Lassie wrinkled her nose, whined, and searched for Rags's scent.

The little dog had collapsed on top of a pile of plastic drop cloths, panting. When Lassie approached him, he rolled on his back and wriggled, all four legs waving like an upside down bug. Lassie nosed the little dog, snuffling his familiar scent. Rags wriggled delightedly. Lassie gave him a swipe with her tongue. As she pulled back, a heavy gauge wire that was sticking out from one of the crates slid under her leather collar and snagged her.

The strong wire jerked her to a halt. She whined, confused, and twisted her forelegs, trying to break free of whatever strange thing held her. For a moment she choked, the collar cutting into her throat as the front of her body hung in mid air, her back legs scrambling wildly to free her.

She managed to brace her forelegs against a box and prop herself so she could breathe again. But the wire still hooked under her collar. Tentatively Lassie pulled back, but the wire held firm to the wood crate. If she had moved forward the wire could have slipped off the collar and she would be free. But now frightened, she pulled back like any caught dog. The leather collar squeaked like a saddle. Lassie grunted, flinging herself back again and again.

Alarmed, Rags barked for his friend. He stood on the loading dock waiting for Lassie to follow him like always. When she didn't he darted away, searching for Katie.

Katie and Jimmy had walked back inside the hardware

store to see a new jigsaw that Jimmy was thinking about buying for Dad for his birthday. To relax, Dad carved wooden toys and he needed a new saw.

When Rags didn't see Katie, he ran circles around Mr. Madison, yipping.

"Is that a dog?" joked the truck driver. "I thought it was a dust ball until it made noise."

"Rags, be quiet," said Mr. Madison. But the little dog continued yapping until Mr. Madison finally picked up the squirming bundle and shut the dog in the bathroom. Rags kept up his rapid fire barking, but it was muffled.

"See you next week," said the truck driver as together he and Mr. Madison heaved shut the heavy truck door, pulled the bolt, and locked it.

The truck engine growled. In the truck's dark belly, Lassie struggled against the wire. The truck ground forward out of the bay and clattered onto the street.

Rags suddenly fell silent, then erupted in a mournful howl.

"Fool dog," muttered Mr. Madison as he went to get Katie to tell her to take her idiot pup home.

Trapped!

Mr. Madison found Katie with Jimmy in the tool section looking at jigsaws.

"Would you do something about your dog?" Mr. Madison asked. "Rags is going nuts. I finally put him in the bathroom."

"Is he hurt?" asked Katie anxiously.

"I don't think so. Probably just bored. Why don't you take him home the long way, hon? You know how Gran is about dogs." Mr. Madison winked at Jimmy to show he didn't have any hard feelings.

Jimmy and Katie scrambled to the back. The bay doors were still open and cool air rushed in. Rags howled from inside the bathroom. When Katie unlocked the door, the dog darted to the edge of the empty truck bay and barked.

Jimmy began glancing around. "Where's Lassie?" he asked and whistled for her. No collie galloped up, tail flagging, eyes begging for attention.

Katie picked up her dog. "What's wrong, Rags?" she

asked and he licked her nose. Then he whined in pitch just like Lassie's common whine for attention.

Jimmy stared at the little dog, then he exchanged a wordless glance with Katie and fear slithered around them.

"Lassie," Jimmy called again and whistled. No tricolored collie appeared. The back lot was empty except for the Madison's truck and Katie's grandmother's Buick. Behind the black, uneven asphalt lay an empty lot where younger kids rode their BMX™ bikes in a makeshift lumpy track. A flock of helmeted boys pedaled past. One of the bikers pulled a wheelie for sheer pleasure.

"Let's go ask them if they saw Lassie," said Jimmy after a minute more of calling. Rags had stopped barking, but lay quiet, most un-Rags-like in Katie's arms. Every few minutes he whined in that unmistakable tone that sound-ed like Lassie.

What was Rags trying to say? Jimmy wished more than ever he could understand dog language.

He and Katie crossed over to the BMX™ track to a clus-ter of kids slouched on their bikes, watching the racers.

❧

Lassie liked riding in cars, but this truck was different. She could tell she was on a highway even though the truck bounced and her head kept hitting against the board where the wire held her. She couldn't pull free of the thing. But worst of all she was being taken from her master.

Jimmy. Her master.

With a half bark, half grunt Lassie once again flung herself back. The collar choked her and cut into her neck, breaking off some of her long hair. The brittle leather of the collar suddenly cracked. The wire passed through and her collar fell off with a jangle of dog tags.

She was free!

She whirled and darted to the truck door, but it was closed. Lassie barked and hurtled herself against the closed metal. She had to get out.

She repeatedly threw her body against the door. But it held fast, a good thing because the truck had turned onto highway 151 to Cedar Rapids and was traveling faster than the 55 mile per hour speed limit. The driver was eager to get home to Des Moines, almost 250 miles from Madison's Hardware Store.

Finally Lassie sunk down, defeated. She rested her beautiful head on her crossed front paws and waited as the truck raced farther and farther away from her Jimmy. Through Cedar Rapids down to Interstate 80 and blasting for Des Moines, the miles shot by effortlessly under Lassie's paws.

❦

"Have any of you guys seen a dog? A big collie?" asked Jimmy.

Faces turned toward him. Tough little faces. *These kids looked like little gangsters,* thought Jimmy. Did I look like that in fourth grade? he wondered.

"A what?" drawled one kid with white-blonde hair.

"Collie," said Katie impatiently. "You know, a big dog with long fur."

They all stared at each other and shrugged. "Nope," said one finally.

"Well, if you do, would you tell someone at the hardware store?" asked Jimmy.

They all shrugged again and he thought they could care less. He and Katie trudged back through the empty lot. Rags still lay in Katie's arms when a kid rode up beside them, flanked by several other kids.

"Hey," he called. "Is your dog the one that came to church?"

Jimmy couldn't help but grin. What would Dad think of that? "Yeah, that's my dog."

The kid nodded. "Cool dog. We'll ask around about her, okay?"

"Thanks." Jimmy and Katie walked back to the hardware store. It was getting dark. Jimmy wondered if someone had stolen his dog. But who? And how? Lassie was wary of strangers and he couldn't imagine she'd willingly get into a strange car or van. She was too big to be easily dragged into a car.

Long ago Dad had taught Lassie never to pick up food unless they gave it to her. He'd put cores of powdered hot peppers in chunks of meat and that cured Lassie from ever picking up food from the ground. So a stranger wouldn't be able to lure her anywhere with food.

He and Katie double checked around the back of the store again, then inside, even opening broom closets and asking people inside if they'd seen her.

Mr. Madison raised his eyebrows. "She's missing? She was just here."

"I know, but she's not now," said Jimmy. He felt sick to his stomach. He was going to have to call Mom because she would be expecting him and Lassie to be home by this time.

All of sudden Jimmy snapped his fingers. He understood why Rags had perched on the back bay and whined like Lassie. "The truck," he said excitedly.

"What?" said Katie.

"That truck delivering stuff here," said Jimmy. The two dogs had been playing around the truck. "I bet she climbed inside the truck and the driver didn't know it."

"How could he shut her in there and not know she was there?" asked Katie.

"I don't know," said Jimmy. "I just don't know."

4

So Near and So Far

It was after five when Jimmy first called Mom, then Dad at church from Madison's office phone. Katie sat on the edge of her father's desk, biting her thumb fingernail. Mr. Madison rifled through a pile of papers while Jimmy explained to his parents that Lassie was missing.

When he hung up Katie asked, "Daddy, can't we call the trucking company? They have radios, don't they? The dispatcher could ask the driver to check his truck."

At least they'd know if Lassie was in the truck or not. Jimmy hadn't tried to explain to his parents what he thought Rags was saying. They'd think he was crazy.

Jimmy held his breath as Mr. Madison put in a call to the trucking company headquarters. *Please God*, Jimmy thought. *Let her be safe in the truck.*

After a few seconds, Mr. Madison made a face and pointed at the clock. "They're closed."

Jimmy groaned.

"Daddy," implored Katie. "We have to do something."

"Honey, I'll call again in the morning. But right now I don't know who else to call."

Jimmy hated being twelve years old. If he was sixteen, he could drive after the truck, flag it down, demand the driver open the back, and see if Lassie was in there. He could bring her home.

But what if they found the trucker and Lassie wasn't in the truck? Where could she be then? What was happening to her?

At five-thirty Mr. Harmon arrived from his office at the church. Together Jimmy, his dad, and Katie walked in widening circles around the hardware store, calling and whistling.

"Maybe she's hurt," suggested Katie. "Hurt animals hide."

"She's too smart to get hit by a car," said Jimmy hating the thought of his dog being run over or struck by a moving vehicle. He couldn't imagine what else would hurt her enough to keep her from returning to him.

But they continued looking until the sun had set completely and it was too dark to see. The wind came up and Jimmy shivered wishing he had his jacket. His stomach told him it was hungry. But he just couldn't go home and leave Lassie. What if she was hurt somewhere, waiting for him to find her, too weak to answer him?

Jimmy walked alone up and down the sidewalks next to the closed businesses. He called her name over and over until it sounded like a wailing song.

At six-thirty, Katie had to go home. Mr. Madison promised to put up a sign in his store and see if anyone had seen the collie.

A sign, Jimmy thought bitterly. He needed to know now what had happened to her. He sighed. He appreciated their help, but it wasn't enough. He had to find her. He just had to. . . .

But that was out of his control.

Totally.

Mr. Harmon drove up beside him. He opened the passenger door, the very door they'd first taught Lassie to open. "Get in, son. We'll drive around some and look for her."

Jimmy stumbled in, shivering. Dad ran the heater full blast and Jimmy hung his head out the window calling Lassie's name over and over until he croaked her name.

When they got home it was after nine. The night was very still and dark.

⚓

The tool truck slowed. Lassie raised her head. Truck gears ground, shifted, and the engine died. The cab door slammed. Lassie stood, her legs shaky and stiff from cold, and barked. And barked.

The scents curling in through the cracks in the door weren't familiar at all. She barked her commanding, deep, watch dog bark of alarm.

Someone outside called, "You got a dog in there?"

"Not hardly," said the driver.

"Sure sounds like you do."

He cocked his head. It sure sounded as if he did. He shook out his keys, unlocked the door, drew the bolt back, and slowly pulled the handle. The door groaned open.

Lassie uncoiled. Quickly, she sprang out of the truck and into the dark night.

The driver swore, startled. He fell back, thinking the dog was leaping for his throat, until he realized Lassie was a stride away. He recognized the beautiful collie he'd admired back at Madison's Hardware. How in the world did she get in his truck?

"Get that dog!" he shouted.

The collie was fifty yards away and hitting top speed. Her fur flattened back as if a giant hand was stroking her entire body at once. She fled under the lights of the cheap diner and vanished into the darkness.

The driver cursed, got a flashlight, and climbed inside his truck with the light. He couldn't catch her by running after her. He'd have to do something else.

He flicked the beam around until it fell over Lassie's collar. The collar lay curled up against a pallet. He picked up the broken leather and read the tags: Lassie owned by Jimmy Harmon with his address and phone back in Farley.

He glanced at his watch, then went to the pay phone

outside the motel office and dialed the number from the dog's tag.

Jimmy and Mr. Harmon were just walking in the house when the phone rang.

His father picked up the phone in the kitchen. "Hello?" Dad clutched the phone to his ear like a lifeboat. Mom was biting her lip, her hands around a mug of coffee. For once, Sarah had nothing to say. She just stood quietly next to Mom.

Jimmy's heart pounded. It was out of his control, only God knew.

"You did?" His father said, put his hand over the receiver and told them, "The truck driver had her in his truck." He turned back to the phone. His face fell. "Was she all right? Where are you?"

"What's happening?" demanded Jimmy. "Is she hurt?"

Dad put up his hand: Wait.

"I understand," Dad was saying. "Can you tell this to my son? She's his dog."

Dad handed the phone to Jimmy. "Hello?" he said eagerly.

"I'm sorry about your dog," the man with the terrific muscles was saying. "I didn't know she was in the back of my truck. How she got in there, I'd like to know. I stopped to grab something to eat and we heard barking. Before I even opened the door all the way, she was out like a shot."

"So you don't have her?" But he knew the answer. So close, but so far.

"She took off into a field. I couldn't catch her," he said. "Sorry."

"Where are you now?" asked Jimmy.

"Just outside Des Moines."

More than 250 miles away!

"If you don't have my dog, how did you know to call us?" asked Jimmy, afraid he knew.

"Her collar came off somehow. It was in the truck," he said. "You know, your phone number is on it."

Silently, Jimmy handed the phone back to his dad. The men talked a few more minutes, then Dad slowly hung up.

Lassie was 250 miles from home, running scared and with no identifying tags on her. Jimmy put his head in his hands and wished instead he was younger than twelve years old so he could cry like a little kid and wait for his parents to make it better.

Heading Home

Nothing smelled right to Lassie. No smells that marked her city, her neighborhood. No familiar scent of silly Rags chasing around her, barking teasingly, prancing stiff-legged. But worst of all, no Harmon family, no sweaty boy smell.

Lassie ran along the road through a pool of neon lights, harsh and old. She didn't like the strange smells and wanted to flee.

Beside her a tractor-trailer rushed past, air brakes screaming into a curve. Lassie leaped the drainage ditch next to the road and ran up a slight bank, her claws spraying the dirt. She crawled under a split rail fence and paused to draw a deep breath. The smells of domesticated animals rose around her—cattle, sheep, horses. She relaxed a little in their familiarness.

Now, what was a lost dog supposed to do?

She paused, lifting her head, the slim muzzle as aristocratic as any blue-blooded royalty. She was of proud lineage, finely bred by men of old in the British Isles during a time when a dog worked hard beside his master.

Where was Jimmy, her master? Where was her favorite rug where she could curl up and sleep? Lassie felt tired, hungry, and alone. She had to get back to Jimmy.

She paused a long moment in the night wind, listening, her soft ears pricked, the tips bent over in proper collie style. Listening intently to the sounds of the night. This way. This way. They seemed to say.

Jimmy was—where?

She swung her head under the sprinkle of starlight, back and forth, listening, smelling. The spring stars lingered. Orion the warrior, his belt and sword gleaming through the muster of clouds. East and a little north. She turned her body, her tail sweeping against the sweet grasses in the field. Not pure east, no, but a bit north, she decided.

Home was this way. Lassie broke into her smooth, effortless trot.

A cluster of cows with new calves jumped nervously and stared at the dog who passed by them. See? The mother cows motioned to their little ones as if to say: That is a dog. We must watch and obey dogs. But Lassie gave no commands to these cows. She was focused on home.

❧

"But we gotta go now," Jimmy insisted. "In a few hours who knows what could happen to her. Now we know where she is. Where she just was."

"Son," Dad said. The man who comforted many found himself without the words to say to his own son. "It's four or five hours away. Even if we left this instant we couldn't get there until three or four in the morning. And it would still be too dark to look for her. Remember the trucker promised he'd call the local animal control first thing in the morning."

Jimmy clenched and unclenched his hands. He wanted to do something now. Now! Oh, if only he was older.

"We'll leave first thing in the morning," said Mom quietly. "You can skip school tomorrow, can't you? No big tests?"

He nodded his head. Even if he'd had final exams he couldn't possibly concentrate. Not when Lassie was still missing.

He choked, unable to even think the words.

"Can I skip, too?" Sarah chimed in. "I don't have any tests tomorrow either."

"I'm afraid not," Mrs. Harmon responded. "As a matter of fact, you need to get to bed."

"I think it would help all of us if we prayed together and asked the Lord to keep His hand on Lassie," Dad said.

Jimmy nodded his head. He wanted to pray, but right now he just couldn't find the words. How could God let something like this happen? He felt as though he was about to cry.

The Harmons joined hands and Dad prayed words

Jimmy was used to hearing. Words like "we love You" and "we believe that all things are in Your hands." But the only words Jimmy could concentrate on were "keep Your protecting hand on Lassie." At this moment, Jimmy wasn't totally convinced that God could protect Lassie.

"Let's try and sleep," said Dad. "We'll leave at six. I'll set my alarm for five-thirty."

"Don't you have a men's breakfast in the morning?" asked Mom.

"I can get someone to cover for me," Mr. Harmon said as he glanced over at his son, but Jimmy was already on his way up the stairs.

Later in bed, Jimmy stared out his bedroom window. Dark. Cold. What was Lassie doing? Was she scared? Did she think he'd abandoned her? He groaned softly and put his head under his pillow. Why did it hurt so much?

❧

In the pre-dawn a farm stirred. Maggie, the eldest daughter of the Lyles, was home from college, between quarters. She saddled her three-year-old Paint mare, Splash.

Nothing like a ride before the day got started, she thought. Maggie first rode the young horse in the small arena she and her sisters had helped their dad build a few years ago. The Paint mare, mostly white with dashes of black spots, shook her black mane and half reared.

Feisty. That's how Maggie liked her horses. She felt that

way about people, too. She grinned thinking of her boyfriend, Matthew. He was taking a group of inner city kids camping for three days. That was feisty. Cool, too.

She rode the little mare out onto a dirt road along the irrigation ditch separating the pastures. The sun wasn't up yet, but the colors stirred on the east horizon—soft pink, dim saffron, pale scarlet. A leaf fell to the ground and Splash let out a rolling snort. Maggie laughed, a silver sound in the darkness.

"Okay, you silly filly, give me your best." Maggie gave the mare a nudge in the ribs and the horse plunged into a gallop.

Lassie had rested in the deep pasture grasses for an hour, her head on her paws, heavily asleep. The clatter of hooves over dirt startled her. She sprang up, alarmed and disoriented as Maggie and her horse raced down the road.

Even though Splash was always looking for an excuse to spook, she was genuinely surprised by the collie's suddenly wolfish appearance in the grass. The horse slammed on the brakes, dropping her head to stare eye to eye with the stunned dog. In that instant, Splash realized it was only a dog and not the wolf of death, but since she was already in the alarm mode, she decided to make the most of it.

Maggie tried to hang on. Splash bawled like a bronc, bucked once, twice, then in a perfect arc, curved skywards, fishing for the stars.

Lassie wuffed in fear and ducked back down the drainage ditch bank, her white paws sinking in the cold mud.

Splash came down so hard, the ground actually shuddered. Maggie thought her spine would pop out the top of her head. Then she was propelled over Splash's neck and slammed onto the dirt road.

On a Mission

Pain. Lassie winced at the young woman's pain on impact. Splash, being young and foolish, had no such feelings and continued bucking for a few seconds more until she realized her rider was already gone.

The horse's head popped up like a jack-in-the-box. Where was her rider? The reins dangling around her neck like strands of ribbons from a trashed birthday present. Ha! A swift searching glance showed her that her rider was four feet away, sprawled on her stomach.

No apparent threat here. Splash gathered herself to spring away, maybe saunter on down the road to hunt up a square of lovely, fresh grass. Perhaps she would have a nice little roll and get rid of this awful, clinging saddle. Then her thoughts shattered as a blur of a dog appeared in front of her.

The mare's head craned higher. This was the beast who had startled her in the first place. Well, no miserable dog would tell her what to do.

Splash started to whirl away only to find the dog instantly at her heels, darting in, leaping back out of the way. Always seeming to turn Splash back to face Maggie again. Now how had that happened? She hadn't wanted to go back towards her rider.

Maggie groaned and sat up. She took a brief inventory of the damages. No broken bones. That's good.

Splash swerved around Lassie, to head out to the pasture where she knew the cows and calves ate the best grass. Grass that should be for a horse. But that dog hugged her hind hooves and somehow Splash found herself even closer to Maggie.

She didn't want to be caught. It was obvious she wanted to get away, but Lassie wouldn't let her. Splash halted directly before Maggie, blinking her usual wild horse eyes in surprise.

Maggie stood. A little stiffly. She rubbed her backside, then took hold of the young mare's reins dangling under her chin.

"Well, thank you," Maggie said to the dog. "This horse would have been in the next county if it wasn't for you." Lassie wagged her tail.

Maggie checked the saddle girth, then slowly mounted. Splash swung her head towards Lassie and flattened her ears.

Maggie laughed. "Serves you right, Splash," she said. "Now you behave." She pushed the horse into a walk and

Lassie followed, heeling with her muzzle parallel to the horse's elbow.

"Nice dog," said Maggie. "I don't recognize you. Live around here?"

Lassie glanced up at the young woman, enjoying her friendly chatter as warm as sunlight. Lassie walked beside Splash along the irrigation ditch for a mile, then the road turned south.

Lassie couldn't go any farther with her. She paused. The sun had slipped up over the horizon spreading streams of clear light over the fields like banners of glitter.

"You're a beauty," said Maggie. She whistled. Lassie's ears pricked forward. "Come on, girl," called Maggie. "Come with us."

Lassie whined and sat down.

"Got other plans?" asked Maggie. "Okay. I can understand that."

Maggie waved good-bye and urged Splash down the road. Lassie stared after them, then continued north-east, heading into the light.

❦

The Harmons left their home at six a.m. Mr. Harmon had called one of the deacons from church to let him know where he was going and why. Mrs. Harmon had taken Sarah to a neighbor's house to stay before and after school. She also gathered several recent photographs of Lassie.

"We can use these to make flyers to post," she said.

Jimmy grabbed Lassie's water bowl and a small sack of dry dog food with a handful of dog biscuits thrown in. He also had folded into a square bundle her blanket with her leash, and an older collar. Then he had added her toy squeak bone. He had put them all in a paper sack and set them on the backseat of the car next to him.

The Harmons drove along the same highway Lassie had traveled just hours before.

In the dim light, farmland whirled past. The sky and ground looked the same color. Jimmy felt like he was looking at an upside down world. Jimmy tried to pray, but his thoughts turned dry and cottony, like pictures of the dust bowl he'd seen in social studies. No words flowed from his brain. Only a picture, like a still shot, of his dog frozen in stride in an unknown backdrop.

Then like a burst of rain a verse flowed over Him, one he never quite understood. Until now. ". . . The Spirit helps us in our weakness. We do not know what we ought to pray, but the Spirit himself intercedes for us with groans that words cannot express" (Romans 8:26, NIV). His Sunday school teacher had said that sometimes the things we pray for go so deep or hurt so bad that we can't even put into words to God how we feel. Then the Spirit of God helps us to pray when we don't have the words.

Groans.

So deep.

That's how Jimmy felt. No one really understood how it felt to lose a best friend, one who was at your side nearly every minute, except when you were in school or church.

As Jimmy listened to the consistent hum of the engine, he felt way down inside that Someone did understand. Someone who could keep Lassie safe from harm. Someone who could bring Lassie back to him.

❧

Lassie trotted all morning along quiet roads. Fields and pastures rolled under her feet. She passed two-story farmhouses, sturdy, weather worn. She passed trees flushing with green buds. She passed small birds busy about nest making, darting over her head, chattering. She saw and heard them all, but they didn't make the slightest difference to her. Nothing mattered but going home.

She was weary. Water had been ample, but food was a different story. She hadn't had any dinner last night and nothing to eat today. Hunger gnawed at her belly, something she really hadn't contended with before. Jimmy had always provided the food.

Lassie stayed on roads along the fields. She knew better than to cross the huge asphalt roads where cars and trucks screamed by, like the road the truck had taken her on last night. If she approached a group of businesses and heavy traffic, she detoured, choosing to pace along the soybean and oat fields or take her chances in a field filled with cattle.

So her first day of wayfaring took her thirty miles, but because of her meandering route, she was only fifteen miles closer to home.

Dusk tumbled down around her, soaking the color from her handsome coat. Car headlights flashed over her and caught the gleam of her eyes like a wild animal's quick gaze.

With the heat vanishing, scents were easier to follow later in the day. They crisscrossed like many threads in a skein, and followed the contours of the land, pooling in depressions close to the ground.

As Lassie jogged down a hill, she caught the scent of cooking meat. Broiling meat with the chunky charcoal smell and spicy barbecue sauce. Must be a restaurant. Not very close. Besides, she knew people didn't take kindly to a stray dog, so she didn't follow the delicious meat scent.

She caught another smell. She sniffed and sniffed. It beckoned her off course just a little. She slowed, hesitating, tempted. Her stomach contracted in hunger. The scent hooked her and reeled her along. Through the darkness she slipped into a small farmyard.

Caught Again

Jimmy got an idea about a hundred and fifty miles into the car trip. It wasn't an idea about homework, either. Mom had made him bring his school books and notebook, as if he could study while Lassie was missing.

Instead he opened his notebook to a blank page, found a pencil, chewed on the eraser for a few minutes, then began to write. He wrote and scratched out, sighed loudly, wrote some more, then rewrote sentences. English was not his favorite subject. He asked Mom how to spell a couple of different words, then recopied his work onto a clean page. When he was done, he said, "Listen to this." He read:

"My collie, Lassie, was accidentally taken near Des Moines. She is loose somewhere nearby. She is a tricolor rough collie. Her fur is long; she's black and tan on all four legs and so is most of her face. She has a lion's mane of white and tan fur and a white blaze.

"She is smart and knows her name. She

49

will come, heel, sit, lie down, and stay on command. She can open car doors, too.

"She saved my life once when I was ten years old. I was playing with friends and an avalanche of snow collapsed off a roof and buried me. She found me and dug me out. I would have died without her.

"Please call----," and he gave their home number because it had an answering machine—"and I will send you a reward of $350 if you find her."

He finished reading. He thought a reward would encourage people to take the time to look for Lassie and make an effort to catch her and call him. All the money he had was in his savings account from working hay mowing jobs during the last two summers. This money was ear-marked for college. But Lassie was more important than college.

He waited for his parents to comment, but they sat in silence. That puzzled him. Maybe they didn't understand why he wrote the paragraphs.

"I thought I could put this in the local newspaper, like in the classified ads or something."

Mom sniffed loudly. Dad's hands were tight on the steering wheel.

"That's a good idea, Jim," he said in a hoarse voice. "We'll find out the name of the daily newspaper in Des Moines and see if they'll print it."

Carefully Jimmy put the paper in his notebook and closed it, then closed his eyes. Memories of Lassie flashed across his mind.

Dad didn't like to emphasize the celebration of Halloween because of its bad pagan roots, so at church they always held a party on Halloween and called it a harvest party. They had games like a cake walk for older kids and a cupcake walk for little kids. They gave out tons of candy. Booths like at a carnival were run by various church families.

Last year Jimmy had helped in the face painting booth. Of course, Lassie came to the harvest party and Jimmy had painted Lassie's face with bright colors, too, so she looked like a clown! The kids laughed and wanted their faces painted like Lassie's.

Close to noon they drove into the outskirts of Des Moines.

"There's the diner the trucker called from," announced Dad. They pulled over and scrambled out. A flashing light read: Eat Good Food.

Jimmy ran across the quiet road to the field where the trucker said Lassie had bolted. He stood on the split rail fence, not realizing she had crept under the boards at his feet. The field stretched for acres. He cupped his eyes from the sun and studied the area.

If he were Lassie, where would he go? Would he hide in the field? It was just an alfalfa field only about knee high. Maybe she would have some mice or rabbits to eat, but as far as he knew Lassie had never caught anything. She was a guard dog. Her ancestors protected sheep, cattle, and even flocks of fowl, as well as humans. She wasn't bred to hunt food and to kill.

He didn't think she'd stay in the field long. She'd strike out on her own. She would head home. To the north east. He turned his body on the fence so the sun struck his right shoulder.

Home. He just knew it. Lassie would head home. She might not understand how far it was but she'd go until she got there.

He jumped down from the fence and ran back to his parents who had gone inside the diner. He opened the door and found them talking with the hostess.

When Jimmy stood beside Mom, she handed him Lassie's broken collar, the tags jingling softly.

Jimmy took it in his hands, not able to look at it, then thrust it deep in his jeans' pocket.

The hostess couldn't tell them much. She only came on duty at eight that morning. Last night the trucker had left a note with his name and address and a scrawled apology with the evening diner hostess.

"Nice of him," said Dad. "Thanks," he said to the clerk and they all went outside.

"That girl told us the big newspaper is THE DES MOINES TIMES," said Mom. "We can head over there and put in an ad. I want to find a copy store, too, and make flyers."

"How about some lunch?" asked Dad. "Breakfast was too long ago."

Lunch. Jimmy swallowed hard. Lassie would be hungry by now. She hadn't had any dinner last night or anything today, as far as he knew.

"Let's go to the newspaper first," Jimmy said. "I want to get the ad in right away."

⚓

Lassie approached the dirt drive of the farmhouse. It was spattered with gravel and deeply rutted. Sagging chain gates yawned open. A human would be suspicious of such a rundown place. Lassie might have been, too, but right now she didn't pay much attention to that. The smell of cooking food drew her. She realized the food was inside a small, one-story house and to get any food she'd have to be invited. She turned away. Another scent, growing stronger was that of many other dogs.

Lassie sneezed and stopped outside a window of the small house. Several humans were inside, even children which was usually what she preferred. She pricked her ears to the cry of a baby. A harsh voice called and the children fell silent. Lassie moved on.

Across the dirty yard was a barn. Behind the barn were the dogs. Many dogs. She could feel them moving in the darkness, stirring to her presence.

Silently she circled around the barn. Kennels of wire mesh ran behind the barn like rows of crops. A couple of nearby dogs began to bark at her. Then more dogs picked up her presence and barked.

The barn door banged open and light poured out. "What's going on?" bawled a man. "Shut up! Miserable beasts."

Lassie cowered as the man's burning gaze stung her.

"Hey, Jack. Get the pole and come here."

A second man joined the first in the barn doorway. Lassie stared back at them, caught like a deer in head-lights. Confused, tired, uncertain of this place. All the dogs. She'd never smelled, never seen so many dogs in one place before.

"Here, poochy, poochy," called Jack.

"She's valuable, I bet," said the first man. "I can sell her over to old Ike. He raises collies. I bet I could get five hundred for a female collie like that."

"Come here, poochy," crooned Jack.

Lassie resisted the command. She didn't like the way the man was creeping at her. She flattened herself out, but hesitated because of the food smell, the dogs, the overwhelming tiredness. Jack drew closer, his hand holding the pole over her head, his other hand outstretched to her nose. Lassie backed away.

"Just pole her," said the first man.

The second man straightened up, dipped the pole like a bat over her. Lassie froze. Behind her dogs hollered. Danger! Here was danger! She gathered herself to leap when steel snapped and a noose clamped around her neck.

She flung herself backwards, but like the wire in the truck, the noose of rope held. She was caught.

8

An Ad in the Times

"**M**aybe someone really nice has found her," said Jimmy. He and his parents waited at the ad desk in the offices of the Times. The paper had a large circulation with both evening and morning editions. He'd run ads in both.

A girl with burgundy-shaded hair and long nails the color of ashes, stood behind the counter. She chewed a huge wad of purple gum. He could see the purple mass each time she popped her gum.

"Can I help you?" she asked.

Jimmy handed her his neatly written page. "How much would this ad be?"

She glanced at it, counted each line, stabbing them with a long nail. Jimmy watched fascinated. How could this girl do anything with nails that long? Except maybe surgery with her nails as scalpels.

"Each line is a buck," the girl informed him. "You've got fifteen lines here. Fifteen bucks a day. Twenty bucks if it runs in evening and morning editions."

Jimmy swallowed hard. "I don't think I can afford that. Just a minute."

He went over to his parents. They conferred and they wrote a shorter classified ad:

Lost: Tricolored, long furred . . .

"Most people don't know the difference between the rough and smooth coated collie," said Dad. "Let's just call her long furred."

. . . female Collie. No collar. Responds to Lassie. Reward.

They also wrote down their home number and the church's number in case their number was busy.

The long nailed girl walked up behind Jimmy. She snapped her gum loudly. "Can I see your story again?" she asked.

He silently handed her the paper. She read it and without lifting her eyes from the page, she said, "I can give this to one of the news editors, if you want. Maybe they can write up a story. More people would probably read that than the classifieds."

"Sure," said Jimmy. "Thanks."

"We've got a photograph, too," said Mrs. Harmon.

"Good." The girl took the photo of Lassie. "Just a minute," she said. She made a photocopy and handed Jimmy back his original. "I'll give these to Mike Evans. He's a nice guy. He does local news."

Jimmy paid money for the ad to run a week in case

they didn't want to do the story. He didn't want to waste any time.

"Here's the classified ad number in case you have to renew the ad," said the girl. "I hope you won't."

"Thanks," said Jimmy.

She paused, tapping a nail, then said, "I have a dog at home. A springer spaniel. If I lost him, I'd just die."

Jimmy nodded. He knew about that.

"Good luck," she said.

※

"Put her in the crate," said the first man.

Jack dragged Lassie, the noose choking her, to a plastic dog crate with a wire front. Together they shoved Lassie inside, pulled the noose off her neck and slammed the crate door.

She'd been in dog crates before. She didn't fear them, but she disliked the two men who smelled dank and musty as an old burrow. They smelled untrustworthy. She backed against the end of the crate as they slid the bolt through the latch.

"I'll go call Ike," said the first man. "Maybe he can come and get her tonight." The men tramped back into the barn and their footsteps carried them on up to the house where the baby had cried.

Lassie uncoiled herself and sniffed the crate. It smelled of many dogs. She pushed against the wire front and it jan-

59

gled a little, but the crate latch didn't budge.

The nearest dog run held a female blonde cocker spaniel and her jumble of puppies. The spaniel laid down parallel to the crate. Lassie and the mother dog stared at each other. The spaniel's deep brown eyes looked sadder than any dog Lassie had seen.

Lassie pushed harder against the crate. She wanted out.

The spaniel whined encouragement. Lassie shoved her shoulder against the crate door and pushed as rain began to fall overhead. The slow, fat raindrops tattooed the earth and rattled on the crate top. Lassie scratched at the corners.

She just had to get out. She just had to.

Rain fell harder, splashing around the crate holding Lassie, filling the dirt ruts. Lassie scratched harder at the plastic corners, but it was sturdy, thick. She pushed her shoulder against the wire mesh and strained. The cocker spaniel had nuzzled her puppies into an overhang out of the rain and then came out to watch Lassie. She whined periodically as if to encourage the collie.

The crate was too strong for Lassie to break.

She paced two steps to the end of the crate, then turned, back hunched, cramped, and paced two steps back to the wire.

She pawed the latch. She pawed it again and again, rattling the bolt. Still it held her prisoner.

Lassie continued to paw at the bolt, raking it downwards. The bolt only jiggled slightly. The cocker spaniel returned to her puppies to feed them, then when they were finished she came back out in the rain to continue her vigil. She whimpered as Lassie pawed the bolt over and over.

In frustration, Lassie backed up and ran the one stride at the mesh. She smashed at the wire door. The whole crate jumped forward. She rammed it. The bolt jumped up when the crate splashed down. Lassie rammed the door. The bolt popped up, then down in the latch.

Lassie was panting despite the cold rain. She rested, only able to hunch in a half sit. Her magnificent white mane was tangled. Bits of of her silky fur had torn out and now clung to the wire door. Lassie backed up like a coiled spring, then shot forward. The cocker spaniel yelped.

The bolt popped up. As the crate was shoved forward, the bolt shifted out of the latch and splashed down into a puddle. The wire door swung open. Lassie all but fell out. She gathered her legs under her and sprang from the crate.

She was free! Free!

9

Unexpected Help

After eating a quick lunch, Jimmy studied the map they'd looked at during lunch. They were driving around in ever widening circles from the point Lassie had last been seen.

At a copy store, they made copies of a flyer with the vital information that Mrs. Harmon had drawn up. She had pasted a photo of Lassie in the upper left hand corner. They made one hundred copies.

As they drove their circles, Mr. Harmon would stop at stores and post offices and other places where many people came and went. Jimmy would hop out and tack up a flyer. He was getting pretty good at the whole routine.

Apparently, a big circus was coming to town soon because he saw posters of clowns and elephants just about everywhere he went. He usually tried to tape his flyer by a circus poster figuring that if people were drawn to the circus poster, they would automatically see his flyer too.

As Jimmy traced his finger on the map he said, "I think Lassie would head for home. This way." He leaned over the car seat and showed Mom on the map a more rural road that headed north east.

"How would she know which way to go, honey?" asked Mrs. Harmon.

Jimmy shrugged. "I don't know, but dogs do, don't they, Dad?"

"Sometimes," said Mr. Harmon. "At least you read stories about dogs who find their way home over hundreds of miles."

Jimmy nodded. He was certain that Lassie was one of the dogs that could do that and she was probably at this moment traveling home. But how long would the trip take her?

He and Lassie had run a 5K run last summer and it took them twenty-five minutes. Of course, Lassie could have run much faster than he. So say it took her a half hour to trot four miles, that would mean she could travel eight miles an hour. To make it easy, say ten miles an hour.

She was 250 miles from home. That meant, let's see. He calculated quickly in his head. Twenty-five hours. Just a little over a day. But could Lassie keep up a pace like that? What if she couldn't go straight home? What if buildings or freeways blocked her way? What if someone captured her? What if she became injured? The "what ifs" stirred around his brain like a maddening stew. So many terrible things could happen to her.

Oh God, please bring Lassie safely home.

A couple hours ago, in a country store someone had asked him who was missing. When he said it was his dog that was missing, an odd look crossed the lady's face, clearly saying, A dog? Big deal. Lassie wasn't like a person missing, but still she was important.

As they drove through rows of houses in a small town, Mrs. Harmon asked suddenly, "Remember when Lassie chased off that intruder?"

"Lassie sure scared him," Jimmy prompted, even though he hadn't been there, but the re-telling was a familiar family story.

"That she did. She wasn't more than a big puppy then," said Mrs. Harmon. She chuckled. "It wasn't the least bit funny then, but it is now."

Mom had been home alone during the day, sewing in the spare bedroom when Lassie came in from the living room, growling, her hackles rising. Mom had looked out the small window to the backyard where a man dressed in jeans and a flannel shirt was at the back kitchen door.

Jimmy was pretty proud of his mom. She had opened the side garden door and quietly told Lassie, "Go get him."

Lassie had burst out, barking. Startled, the man fled, leaping for the top of their wooden fence. But not before Lassie had torn off a piece of his flannel shirt. She'd trotted back to Mom, the blue and red striped material flapping in her mouth. Jimmy smiled a little, remembering Mom showing him the material. For days when they showed the flannel piece to Lassie, she'd growl and snap at the fabric.

❧

Lassie faded into the deeper shadows of the barn. Over the rattle of the rain on small leafed trees, the murmur of voices came from the house. Children shouted. A woman whined. The voices of the two men yelled back and forth.

Lassie laid back her ears and followed the wonderful scent of dog food. Fifty pound bags of Kibble lay in a lean-to next to a row of kennels. Lassie tore open a bag and ate a few quick mouthfuls, only pausing to listen, to watch for her captors.

The spaniel softly whined several times and Lassie's calm eyes studied the dog, her puppies, the kennel. When she had eaten her fill, she went up to the spaniel mother and her puppies.

Lassie hesitated, then went to the door of the kennel. A few dogs behind her barked. She'd better hurry. She reared up on her hind legs, nosed at the latch, then grasped the bolt in her teeth and pulled. The bolt slid out. Lassie dropped it in the mud.

Then she dropped down on all fours and trotted into the sheets of rain. Just before rounding the barn, Lassie looked back. The cocker spaniel was nudging her puppies out of the kennel.

Lassie whined low in her throat, then she was off, running out of the muddy barnyard, leaping the fence and flying across a plowed field, glad the wet dirt scent was stronger than the kennel stink she left behind.

The clouds blotted out the stars. But Lassie didn't hesitate. She continued north east, trotting strongly, revitalized by the food and the sweet taste of freedom.

❧

The Harmons drove down a quieter road lined with young growing alfalfa. Several horses stood in a dirt paddock near the road. One, a splashy Paint mare, flung up her head as their car passed.

At dusk they stopped to eat dinner in a small family restaurant called the Charming Chicken.

Jimmy asked if he could post a flyer and he was allowed to do so. The Harmons bought the evening paper. The classified wasn't due to run until tomorrow morning, but on the bottom of the local news front page was Lassie's picture and two columns of copy. The headline read: Boy Searching For Collie

"Awesome," said Jimmy. His story appeared just as he'd written it, his handwriting and all. The newspaper had photographed his written page and shrunk it down. The word *Reward* was at the bottom of Lassie's photograph as if Lassie was a Most Wanted criminal. Jimmy grinned.

"That girl was nice to pass on your story to the news editor," said Mrs. Harmon.

"I'll say," said Mr. Harmon. "Talk about an answer to prayer."

Jimmy hoped that tonight someone would find Lassie and call about her. That would save her from having to travel home. It was just too dangerous for her. Too much could happen to her. Cities, traffic, and stuff.

Carefully he tore out the story, folded it, and put it in his wallet.

After dinner Mr. Harmon called the answering machine at home, but the only messages were from Katie, several members of church, and some other friends at home.

Mr. Harmon re-dialed the answering machine and held the phone out to Jimmy. "Listen to Katie's message," he said.

Jimmy listened. Katie's voice said, "Hi, Harmons. I wanted to let you know about those kids Jimmy and I talked to, you know, on the bikes behind our store? They came over to tell us to tell you that they are praying for Lassie to come home. They actually divided up the day by hours and assigned different kids to pray. Even at night. Can you believe it?"

Jimmy dazedly handed back the phone. He didn't even hardly know those kids. Awesome, really, awesome.

10

New Hope

That night the Harmons found a small motel about fifteen miles from where Lassie was last seen. They continued to post flyers, and even had to find another copy store to make additional copies. But at eight-thirty the rain began to pour down, so they drove back to the motel.

Mrs. Harmon thought, *poor Lassie . . . somewhere out in this rain.*

Mr. Harmon felt bad for his family. Everyone was worrying about Lassie and he felt very frustrated because he couldn't do anything to make it better.

Jimmy hoped she didn't get mixed up on her way home. Would the rain mess up scents or whatever it was that guided her home?

Before they went to bed they prayed together for Lassie. But it was a long time before Jimmy could fall asleep. He tossed and turned, sleeping fitfully.

Later that night, Jimmy awoke. His parents' breathing was slow and deep. His father snored occasionally. Jimmy reached out from under the covers and pulled back the curtain. Outside the rain continued to fall; the sky was blank and mushy with shapeless clouds. His lips whispered a prayer as the curtain swung back into place and finally he slept again.

Early the next morning the Harmons drove up and down farm roads. Mr. Harmon phoned home. No new messages. They stopped at a fast food restaurant, bought breakfast and the newspaper. Their ad ran along with a dozen other lost dog and cat ads.

"How sad," said Mrs. Harmon. "What happens to all those lost pets?"

Jimmy didn't want to think about it. He wanted to do something to find Lassie. "I'm done eating. I'm going to put up a flyer, okay?"

The sleepy farm community looked boring. Jimmy wished there was some way to ride a flying scooter or something. He could zoom along zipping in and out of farm yards, searching quickly for his dog. Too bad he couldn't ask an angel to sweep along and search for Lassie.

Suddenly, he thought he saw her. He yelled frantically, pointing out the window. "Dad. I think I see her over there! There! Do you see her?"

A dog jogged along an irrigation ditch. A long furred black, gold, and white dog, Lassie's colors. But it didn't move right somehow. No, it wasn't tall enough, the legs

were too short. Not Lassie. It looked like some kind of collie mix.

When they got closer, Mr. Harmon pulled up slowly.

"Poor dog," murmured Mrs. Harmon.

Jimmy called out the window, "Hey, dog." The dog
spooked at his voice and rocketed over the ditch and disappeared into a clump of weeds.

They drove on silently in the drizzle.

❧

Lassie traveled most of the night, resting under some
trees with a clump of yearling steers, protected somewhat
by the leaves. The young cattle had lowered their eyes and
stared at her, but didn't run. She didn't attempt to bother
them, but merely curled up next to the trunk of a tree,
among soft leaves and slept.

As the sun came up, Lassie stood and stretched, arch-
ing her back. The young steers jumped and rolled their big
eyes at her. She merely yawned, showing white teeth,
drank some rainwater from puddles among leaves, then
moved into a lope, leaving the young steers behind.

❧

About one in the afternoon the Harmons stopped to eat
and phone home again. Mr. Harmon's face lit up.
"Someone has seen Lassie!"

Jimmy dashed to the phone. His dad quickly passed the
phone to Jimmy, pressing the receiver against his ear.

On the message tape, a girl's voice was saying, "It was a collie, like your story said. She startled my horse yesterday morning and I was bucked off. My horse is kind of an idiot. When my horse tried to take off, the dog wouldn't let her. She actually moved the horse up to me. It was kind of amazing. The dog followed me for a while, but when I turned back to go to my house, the dog followed Bishop Creek, going north. I hope this helps you." She gave her address and phone number.

Jimmy's face was shining. "I bet that was Lassie. That's what she'd do!"

"Don't get too excited," warned Dad. "Remember, we just saw a dog that looked kind of like Lassie."

"But that dog ran off," said Jimmy. "Lassie wouldn't do that. I bet it was Lassie!" Helping a girl with her horse was a Lassie kind of thing!

Mom put her hand on Jimmy's shoulder and squeezed gently. "Maybe it was Lassie, honey. We'll keep looking."

As Jimmy climbed back into the car, he wondered grimly what would happen if they hadn't found her by Sunday night. Dad had arranged for one of the church deacons to preach for him tomorrow morning and evening. He'd already missed one day of school. Would his parents let him miss another, and another? How long would his parents drive around looking, staying in motels, even though the motels were fairly cheap. They didn't have money to keep eating out and paying to stay in rooms when they had a perfectly good house in Farley.

Again he hated being just twelve years old. What a drag! He couldn't do anything by himself. It was like being a second rate citizen. Unfair. He reminded himself that when Jesus was twelve years old, He was talking about God and stuff in the temple with the priests. They treated Him like, like, He was a grown up and they respected Him and what He had to say.

Jesus must have sounded impressive and clear thinking. Jimmy decided he needed to act like that, too. Not kid-like and whining about Lassie. He was being responsible in looking for her because she was his responsibility. Also, it was his fault that she got on that truck. Not really, really his fault because it was an accident. But still it was kind of his fault because he was supposed to be watching her. If he acted like Jesus had, grown up and reasonable—although he knew a lot of grown-ups who weren't always reasonable—then maybe his parents would let him continue to look for her.

He pressed his nose against the glass and kept searching the passing countryside.

A Boat Ride on the River

The rest of the day Lassie steadily headed north east. Clouds remained dark and lightning stabbed the distant Dubuque Hills. Twice she had to cross rivers, fast moving rivers, full from the not long ago snow and ice melt. The first river she crossed on a pedestrian bridge, dodging mountain bikers skimming over the river as fast as the river flowed underneath. One mountain biker yelled at her. She swerved to the side of the bridge, wondering if she should jump down and swim the rest of the way.

No, the drop was too far and the river too fast. Instead she flattened herself against the side of the wooden bridge, waited for the line of bikers to pass, then hurried off the bridge. She scrambled down, relieved.

The next bridge, however, was more of a problem.

It was a four lane road with no shoulders. A big sign read: Narrow Bridge. But she didn't need to know how to read to figure that out. She paused on the dirt path that led up from the river to the bridge's edge. Wind rushing from the passing cars and trucks ruffled her long, tangled coat. Her once tidy white paws were streaked with mud. She lifted her narrow muzzle. Lassie watched and waited patiently as cars streamed by unrelenting.

Once during a lull of traffic she began to cross the bridge, hugging the side of the first lane, but she stopped short when a truck blasted its airhorn. She yelped and leaped over the edge of the bridge into the soft mud.

Should she try again? Nervously she stood hock deep in water trying to judge if it would be safe to try again.

A whistle cut through her concentration. Lassie looked downstream. A girl stood near a small outboard motorboat. She had a fishing net in her hand, the boat's tow rope in her other hand. Already in the boat was a small boy. He was complaining, "Bridget, let's go. I want to go home."

"Here, girl," called Bridget and whistled again, ignoring her pesty little brother. "Don't cross that bridge. It's not safe." She snapped at the boy, "Give me some of that bacon."

He tossed her a slimy piece of bacon they'd been using for bait.

"Here girl, come and get it," coaxed Bridget.

Lassie smelled the bacon and she liked the girl's gentle voice. It reminded her of Katie. The boy was about the age of Jimmy when Lassie had first come to the Harmons as a puppy. Slowly she waded out of the river's edge and walked along the narrow sandy path. She sat in front of the girl and waited.

"You're a beauty," said Bridget. She tossed the bacon and Lassie caught it with a snap.

"Beauty?" said the boy. "She's about as messy as a dog can get. She needs a bath."

"So do you, Nicholas," retorted Bridget. "Should I leave you behind because of it? She wants to cross the bridge. If she'll come in the boat, we can take her across."

The boy rolled his eyes. "How do you know she wants to cross the bridge?"

"Didn't you just see her? She tried to cross the bridge, but that truck scared her. It's too narrow anyway. It's not safe." Bridget reached out and Lassie allowed her to stroke her head.

"Give me some more bacon," said Bridget.

Nicholas threw Lassie another piece and the collie caught it neatly. Gently Bridget slapped her leg and called to Lassie. Lassie got up and came to the boat prow. The water slapped the painted wood. Bridget rewarded her with another bacon slice.

"Come on in," Bridget coaxed.

When Lassie put a foot on the boat prow, it rocked and she pulled back. "It's okay," said Bridget and she hopped out and stepped back in to show her. "See? The boat just rocks."

Nicholas sat, hand on the starter, and rolled his eyes again. "Bridget, that dog doesn't understand what you are saying."

Bridget turned on him. "How do you know what dogs can or can't understand? Besides she's smart. You can tell. Just look at her face."

Nicholas snorted.

Bridget coaxed Lassie forward again. She knew better than to force the dog in the boat. Finally, Lassie placed a paw on the rocking prow again. Bridget patted her head encouragingly. "That's it, come on, girl."

Finally Lassie hopped inside, her back legs tense, ready to spring out of this strange thing the children sat in. Bridget patted the wooden bench and said, "Sit here."

Lassie knew the word sit and obeyed, perching awkwardly on the bench. Then Bridget sat next to the dog and put her arms around the soft fur. "Engage the helm," commanded Bridget.

Nicholas stuck out his tongue at her, but started the outboard engine.

"Proceed to warp one," said Bridget. Nicholas did as she said and the boat growled away from the shore. Lassie whined anxiously as they roared onto the river.

"Don't worry," said Bridget. "We're experienced space dogs." She laughed at her joke.

Lassie whined, but remained trustingly against Bridget's thin side.

❦

"Remember how Lassie was so scared of water?" said Jimmy. "But she learned it was okay." She never quite got into swimming like a pointer or a springer spaniel dog did. But on summer vacations he had coaxed Lassie to come swimming with him along the shore of Lake Superior. Those were the days. Endless twilights, warm sand, cool water. Sometimes very cold water. Just being together. . . . that's what really counts.

That night he and his parents called it quits about seven. They stopped at a supermarket and bought some fruit, cheese, bread, and juice. Jimmy added two cans of Lassie's favorite dog food to the shopping basket.

His parents exchanged glances.

"She'll be hungry when we find her," he protested and then with a shock realized his parents didn't think they'd find Lassie.

He grew quiet, afraid. His father was a man of God. If he thought something was beyond hope . . . .

No. Everything his parents had told him and everything that he understood about God was to never give up hope. Like King David praying for his baby not to die. Everyone thought the king was nuts to believe the baby would be spared. Yet he believed the baby would live until the baby was actually gone.

That was it, wasn't it? That God could do anything, even if it seemed impossible. So you didn't so much look at the circumstances, but believed God would go beyond the circumstances. You hoped.

Jimmy also knew God didn't make everything better

just because you wanted that. A lump rose in Jimmy's throat. He knew that. He wasn't such a baby to think that whatever he wanted, God would make happen. He'd been disappointed before. Lots of times.

Like when some guys beat him up at school a couple years ago.

Like when Grandpa died when he was in fourth grade.

Like when his bike was stolen and his parents couldn't afford to replace it for more than six months.

The list could go on and on.

But Lassie seemed, what? Different. She had been such a gift, such a wonderful, magical thing in their lives. So why would God take her now? In just a few years, dogs being the way they are, she'd be an old dog. That wasn't so long from now. Why not let her stay with them until then? He just didn't know.

The Harmons ate dinner in their motel room, the evening news blaring depressing stories on the television.

Jimmy felt his parents' worried gazes on him like flies landing. He didn't like this change in them. He wanted them to be like King David, praying and hoping until it was obvious that what had happened was permanent.

But Lassie being gone was not permanent. Not yet.

A Silent Shadow

Bridget and her brother motored Lassie south a half mile down the river. She was restless, not wanting to be carried off course. She whined and leaned against the side of the boat until Bridget was afraid that the big dog would leap into the water.

"Don't worry," said Bridget. "We're taking you to the edge of the park. If we took you directly across that bridge, you'd be right at the highway interchange. You wouldn't like that, would you?"

Lassie listened intently. Even though she did not understand what the girl was saying, Lassie detected that she had found a friend, someone who had fed her and showed her kindness, someone like Jimmy. It made her long for home.

Nicholas cut the engine and the small boat bumped up against the shore. He sprang out, grabbed the tow rope and tied it around a sapling.

"Come on, girl," said Bridget. "Now you can get out of the boat."

Lassie hopped over the side and onto the sandy shore. Bridget dumped out the last of their cut bacon pieces for the dog. Lassie nosed the slices of meat, then swallowed them gratefully.

Bridget laid a gentle hand on the dog's head and began stroking her fur softly. "I don't know where you are going, but wherever it is, be careful. I wouldn't want anything to happen to you." Bridget paused for a moment, not really wanting to say good-bye. Finally, she said, "Go."

At the word *go* Lassie pricked up her ears and whined. "Go," Bridget repeated softly.

Lassie understood that command. She turned and trotted off across the sand, up to a wide hiking path on the edge of the regional park.

"You're crazy, Bridg," said Nicholas. "That was an expensive dog. You could have sold her or something."

Bridget gave him a disgusted look. "She's going somewhere. I couldn't stop her."

"Have you heard of a leash?" he asked as they got back in the boat.

Bridget didn't answer. She could tell that the dog was heading somewhere important to her and it was enough that she'd been able to help her. Once her old granny told her that angels could disguise themselves as people or as animals. Perhaps this dog was an angel unaware that they had helped.

"God speed," she whispered, but the roar of their outboard engine starting up drowned out her voice.

❀

Lassie trotted through the huge, empty regional park. As dusk floated down on the earth, the stronger scents rose up and snaked around bushes and trees. She smelled rabbits, raccoons, slow moving possums, and coyotes—dogs' infamous brothers.

She also smelled old fires; many, many humans and their pet dogs who'd visited in days past.

Most current, though, was the smell of people who were agitated and fearful. She wondered what they feared for the night was honest and safe smelling to her.

Off to the left, beams of flashlights clicked on and occasionally the murmur of humans reached her, but nothing was directed at her.

"Did you hear something?" a distressed voice whispered.

Lassie stopped.

"Naw, you're just letting this quiet night air get to you," someone responded. "Go back to sleep."

So the park wasn't as empty as she had thought. She made herself as a silent shadow in the night as she continued her journey across the wide park.

Once she halted to sniff her wild brothers' trail. They were a mated pair. Their paths crisscrossed with human and rabbit. They were nothing to her so Lassie lifted her head and continued on her own errand. She longed for home. And she would make it, no matter what.

❧

Jimmy took a long shower. He was exhausted.

Once when he and Lassie had been out walking in the fields outside of town, a breeding bull rose up from a clump of bushes where it had been resting. Bulls are nothing to mess with. If Jimmy had known it was in the field, he never would have crossed the field, no matter how short the short cut.

The bull bellowed and pawed a warning into the ground, hiking dirt up over its thick, broad back.

Someone had told Jimmy once that if a bull charged, he should freeze, but that was easier said than done.

The bull suddenly sprang forward. The huge bulk headed right for him, traveling faster than Jimmy thought possible for its size. Without any hesitation, Jimmy burst into a run. The fence line was much too far away even for him and he had always thought of himself as a good runner. So he flew for the trees.

The bull cut diagonally across the field, dust billowing up as if a herd of cattle was charging him.

Jimmy realized he'd never make it to the trees either.

Suddenly Lassie appeared as if dropped in by parachute. She dove at the bull's tender nose and slashed his muzzle. The bull bellowed in pain. Lassie darted out from under his furious sweep of horns. Then she zipped around to the bull's heels, biting at his hocks, driving him mad.

The bull forgot about the boy. He whirled around to face the dog, but the dog was gone. The bull lifted his head, his little, mean eyes hunting.

Lassie erupted, biting his shoulder. The bull kicked mightily, grazing Lassie's neck. It must have hurt, but she never made a sound. She just continued to slash at the monster, distracting him, as Jimmy veered from the trees and ran for the fence. He tried to imagine that he was stealing home-base.

Lassie continued snapping, teeth clicking at heels, hocks, nose. The bull bellowed and stomped, trying to smash the dog.

Jimmy reached the fence, climbed over and began calling his dog. "Lassie! Come," he shouted. "Come, girl." But Lassie did not come.

"Oh, God, don't let the bull hurt her," he prayed quickly, almost unconsciously. He felt powerless to help her. He just stood, watching, his fists clenching and unclenching, dying a thousand times, each time as the bull kicked and drove horns at his dog.

But she dodged skillfully—twisting, leaping—and suddenly Jimmy understood the incredible wisdom that God had given animals. Lassie knew exactly what she was doing even though she had never herded cattle before. Her ancestors had been carefully bred for the best of the best herding instincts and somehow that knowledge deep within was now awakened.

He marveled at her dangerous ballet. Finally, she glanced up to see that he was safe, then she slipped away from the bull and dashed for the fence. The bull started after her, but in a moment gave it up. He probably didn't want to deal with any more slashing bites.

Jimmy hugged Lassie for a long time. "I can't believe you went after that monster, Lassie," he said as he hugged her. "You are some dog."

Tenderly he cleaned the abrasion from the bull's hoof that had torn off a strip of fur and skin from her neck. Over time the wound had healed but Lassie still carried the thin scar buried under her fur.

13

Double Trouble

Laura Tyler had just turned five years old. She and her family—Mom, Dad, and two older brothers—had come to the park for a day's outing. Her brothers tossed a football with Dad. Boring.

Laura and her mom had walked along some of the paths gathering wild flowers and bits of odd leaves and small branches. Her mom liked to create natural wreaths and bouquets for a local florist so they did a lot of foraging.

Then Laura and her mom rested on a blanket, her mother eventually falling asleep. Laura picked up one of the foraging bags. She would surprise her mom by finding more stuff for her wreaths. So she'd skipped off down one of the trails of the big regional park in search of interesting wild things.

That was about three-thirty Saturday afternoon, or as near as anyone could figure since Laura's father and brothers were playing such an intense game, they never bothered to look up. When Laura's mother awoke, she realized she was alone. She called Laura's name over and over again, becoming more hysterical with each call.

About four-thirty the sheriff came. Laura's parents and brothers had nearly exhausted their efforts to find the little girl and realized they needed more help. By five p.m., the sheriff's posse and the volunteer search and rescue team had begun setting up their command post. They divided into units and began making grid searches throughout the park.

"Little girl, five years old, light brown hair, grey eyes, name Laura Tyler. Dressed in jeans, pink sweater. Last seen in campsite 14," recited the Incident Command Officer. They had a good print of her tennis shoe, but unfortunately it was a common tread.

"Like fifty million other little kids who come here," commented a searcher dryly.

But they began searching in an organized fashion, two or three people for each grid. The posse rode their horses through the park, depending on their horses to notice a movement they would miss in the dark. Children can hide in the weirdest places, especially if they are scared. Sometimes you can call their names and they won't answer, even if you are right next to them. Who knows little kids' minds? The searchers tried to comb the area carefully, but the park was big and hilly and full of scrub bushes.

Lassie wondered at the commotion of humans crashing through the brush in the near dark. She continued to follow the coyote pair only because they were headed in the direction she was already going. The big dog was vaguely disturbed by the coyotes' emotional charge coming through from their scent. Unusual excitement. She could almost see it like a glowing thread in the wild ones' scents. What were they up to?

❦

"The Center for Search and Rescue reported this afternoon that a small girl has been lost in Black Hawk Regional Park today. Search teams are currently combing the area but have not been successful in locating the child. The child is a five-year-old female with light brown hair and grey eyes. Her name is Laura and she is dressed in jeans and pink sweater. Anyone knowing the whereabouts of Laura is asked to call the Center's office at 739- . . ." The television announcer finished his report and moved on to other local news.

Jimmy had just come out of the shower, rubbing his hair with a towel.

"That's near here," said Mom. "Isn't it?" She lifted the map.

Jimmy didn't care. He just wanted his dog back. If some stupid little kid had wandered off, it was her fault. His dog was taken away on a truck. It wasn't Lassie's fault she was lost.

He knew he was being mean, but he was too tired to

89

care about anything or anyone other than himself and Lassie.

He flung himself on the bed and closed his eyes. Not even praying. He was beyond prayer, beyond anything but that silent groaning down deep in his heart that surpasses understanding.

❦

As she traveled on a trail through the park, Lassie picked up the scent of a child. The scent became stronger as she moved down the trail. Lassie quickened her pace.

Then another scent became strong, a familiar scent, a scent she knew could mean trouble.

In the near dark light, a small child lying on the ground came into view. Near her stood a coyote. Lassie knew the coyotes had to be somewhere, but only one was visible. A cautious, uneasy feeling swept over her.

The she-coyote stood a couple feet from the child who was being kept awake by the cold. She wore a thin pink sweater and had wrapped her arms tightly around herself. She pressed her body against a slight rise in the ground to keep warm, but the rippling wind burned the cold into her little body.

"Go away, doggie," Laura said sternly. She didn't like the way the she-coyote stared at her with intense eyes. The coyote hesitated attacking because the child wasn't acting fearful. Fear was a sharp, almost sweet scent that the coyote knew well.

Lassie trotted faster along the path. As she sped forward, the wild one spotted her. The she-coyote yipped and whirled to face the big dog, a sly glint in her eyes. Normally the coyote would run from a large dog, but she knew something the dog didn't. But she misjudged Lassie.

One summer Lassie and Jimmy had stayed in Montana, prime coyote and sheep country. Oh, yes, Lassie knew something about the wily coyote.

The she-coyote yipped again and slowly moved off down the trail, to lure Lassie. But Lassie knew what was going on. She stopped in front of Laura and turned back the way she had come. Sure enough. The coyote's mate was silently stalking her. An old coyote trick. One distracts and the other sneaks up from behind and attacks.

Lassie stood her ground, snarling. She was much bigger than the other coyote.

The male coyote slid away and the female followed. Lassie stood a moment listening, not convinced they were leaving for good. It wasn't good for a young human to be out alone. She turned to the child and whined.

"You're a nice doggie," said Laura. "I'm glad you told those other two doggies to go away. They aren't nice. I didn't like them."

Lassie put her nose down to Laura and the little girl petted her with cold fingers. Laura didn't hear the crackle of paws, but Lassie did and knew the coyotes were circling, watching. So she did what she had been bred to do. With a sigh she lay down beside Laura. To protect her. That was a law of the collie. To protect.

Laura snuggled up to Lassie. "Good doggie," she murmured. "Are you going to tell me a bedtime story, too?"

Lassie licked the child's dirty cheek and waited.

The night fell silent. Lassie longed to be on her way, but she waited patiently as the child slept. Warmer, but subconsciously still uneasy, Laura cried a little in her sleep, calling for her mother and digging her feet and hands into Lassie's sides like a demanding puppy. Lassie didn't mind and licked the little girl's ear.

About two in the morning two searchers walked the path. They would have walked right by Laura and not seen her, except Lassie had been waiting and heard them. As they approached, she whined loudly. Laura was sleeping more soundly now and didn't awake even as Lassie barked.

A flashlight beam fell over her, blinding her, and a man said, "Look at that. A dog found her."

Lassie moved out of their way and one of the men wrapped the child in a thin space blanket and picked her up, still drugged with sleep.

Lassie's job was over so she turned and disappeared down the trail.

Returning Home

Sunday the Harmons slept later than they had been. Jimmy spent a very restless night. He kept dreaming that he was looking for a lost ring of keys. Which was dumb since he only had one key, his house key.

By eight, the Harmons were driving and searching. Jimmy sat in the backseat with the newspaper. His classified ad was in the paper again. He scanned the other missing pets section.

A four-pound chihuahua named Hugo was missing. A twenty-pound cat named Baby was missing. Jimmy wondered briefly if Baby had eaten Hugo. A pet possum wearing a collar with a tag that read Guido was missing. A yellow parakeet with a band on its leg with the numbers 34732 was missing. A blonde cocker spaniel with her six puppies was missing. *That was different,* thought Jimmy. *Why would a mother dog run away with her puppies?*

In the driver's seat, Mr. Harmon cleared his throat. "Jimmy?"

He put down the classifieds. "Yeah, Dad?"

"Your mother and I have been talking."

Not a good phrase. He had a sick feeling he knew what Dad was going to say.

Dad continued, "We think we should return home tonight. That doesn't mean we can't keep looking for Lassie. We can run the ad longer. Send out some flyers to pet stores and call animal shelters, but we need to get back home."

Go back home without Lassie. He wanted to scream and pound the seat of the car with his fists. He wanted to ask, If I was lost would you give up so easily? But of course, they'd say that's different, Lassie isn't our child. Then he'd say, You always told me that God helps those who help themselves. Doesn't that mean we should keep trying? Not give up? And Dad would say, We aren't exactly giving up. We're still trying, but we have responsibilities at home.

Oh, they'd had this conversation a billion times before. The topic merely varied. It was called parents vs. the kid.

Jimmy said, "Dad, respectfully, I disagree. I think we should continue to look for another day or two. Before the trail gets cold."

Mom turned and stared at him. He nearly grinned. Maybe this acting responsible, like Jesus-the-kid in the temple would work for him, too.

But Mom only said, "I don't know, honey. We've been gone since Friday. Your father needs to get back to work.

We need to check on Sarah. And you need to go back to school."

School wasn't as important as Lassie, but he didn't think he could argue successfully about that point.

"Can you keep looking then?" he asked Mom. It was a logical idea. After all, she didn't have to go to work or school. She looked doubtful.

"No," said Dad. "I don't think it's a good idea for your mother to roam around a strange countryside."

He wanted to ask, Isn't this Iowa? You know, the Midwest? It wasn't like he was asking if Mom could go begging on the streets of Hollywood or something. But he kept his mouth shut because an idea was hatching in his brain.

❧

Lassie came out of the park, sorry to leave behind the gentle trails that were soft on her feet and return to hard packed asphalt. She was getting hungry, too. At dawn she rested for an hour and drank water from a leaking sprinkler system in an office complex. She found a bag from a fast food joint in a trash can and ate the remaining burnt French fries from the bottom of the bag.

Then she traveled on. She shifted upwind, sorting odd and familiar scents. The warm smells of livestock flowed along the air currents, but an even stronger scent was that of animals she didn't know. Some were grass eaters, but not horses or cattle. Some were meat eaters, but not dogs or cats although the scent was reminiscent of mountain lion, something she'd encountered the same summer she met coyotes on the sheep ranch.

By noon Sunday she had reached the animal scents. She stood on the edge of the teeming grassy area, the wind blowing scent and sounds to her. She read them like Jimmy read the classified ads.

Large striped red and white tents were being set up, huge things, the size of houses, smelling of plastic. Trailers and trucks were being unloaded with the harsh gasoline smell. Men and women rushed everywhere, lugging ropes, buckets, grooming tools, carts. Above all were animal smells. Lassie couldn't figure out the odd creatures. Rank scent of cat, not a house cat, but a huge cat. Some kind of enormous leathery creature, smelling of hay.

Curious and hungry, she slipped into the commotion, staying well hidden under trailers, watching with bright eyes.

The other animals knew she was there, but ignored her. A dog. Big deal. They knew about dogs and weren't impressed. Only the chimpanzee, Taber, was curious. He smacked his rubbery lips and stretched his arm through his cage bars.

Lassie lay under an empty stock trailer, which was familiar because horses had been carried in it. Getting no response from the dog, Taber picked up an orange slice and held it out. He smacked his lips. But Lassie didn't react.

So Taber tried a banana. Nope. Then he tried a piece of Kibble dog food left over from his dinner.

Lassie recognized the shape of the Kibble and pricked her ears at the dog food in the primate's long fingered hand. Taber smacked his lips again and waited.

Lassie didn't move until two men with a ladder hurried by, then she crept out from under the stock trailer and crossed the grassy ground to Taber's large cage. It was mounted on a trailer. She'd been watching him for awhile now. He was a funny creature. For he resembled the shape of a man, yet didn't smell manlike nor did he talk like a human. She decided he was an animal, but one to be wary of. Not like a bull or a horse to be bossed around. He required some thought.

She stood before the chimp, her head level with the floor of his cage. He opened his hand and let the Kibble drop to the ground. Lassie sniffed the food, then gobbled it up.

Taber held out a handful, but didn't let it drop this time. Lassie stared longingly after it. Could she trust the creature? Hunger won out and she reared up so her nose was next to the chimp's hairy arm.

She got a good whiff of him. Definitely not human. When the chimp lowered his hand, she ate the Kibble from his hairless palm.

When she finished, the chimp jumped back, chattering. Startled, Lassie dropped back and barked. Taber grabbed the last of the Kibble from his ceramic bowl and held it out. Lassie slowly reared back up, staring into the wrinkled face of the chimp, his eyes bright, intelligent, friendly. Then she dipped her head and ate. When Lassie finished eating, Taber didn't make a sound. She just sat quietly staring at Taber. Lassie didn't drop down to all fours, but watched the chimp closely. She and the chimp gazed at one another and seemed to come to an agreement. Slowly Taber stroked Lassie's head and she allowed his fingers to touch her soft fur.

15

Child Saved By Dog

So Sunday night they drove home. That was just fine with Jimmy. He had made other plans. He slouched in the backseat with a penlight reading the Des Moines Sunday paper. For right now, he didn't want to think any more about his plan.

Elections. Blah. New utility tax. Double blah. Criminal cases. Would he be considered a criminal because of his plan? He wouldn't think of that either.

As he turned the pages, he noticed a full-page circus ad. *There's that circus, again,* he thought to himself. *I wonder how much an advertisement like that would cost?* If he had the money for an ad this size, he probably would have Lassie back by now. He closed his eyes and envisioned how the ad would look. The word *Lassie* in super big type. Her picture blown up in the middle of the page. Maybe his hand written note. Oh, well, no point in thinking about that.

He turned the pages until he came to the local news. A photograph of a little kid wrapped in a blanket being held by a man with a beard. On his baseball cap in neon orange letters was the word *Rescue*. The caption read: "Laura Tyler, 5, was discovered by rescuers approximately 2 a.m. this morning. Rescuers reported that she was being protected by a large stray dog."

He sat straight up. A stray dog! He read the article in a gulp.

Child Saved By Dog and Rescuers

Laura Tyler, 5, had wandered away from her family late yesterday afternoon at Black Hawk Regional Park. Search and Rescue teams were deployed at five p.m. and searched until 2 a.m. when two members discovered the little girl asleep beside a large dog.

Matthew Hoover, 37, a member of the volunteer Upper Iowa Search and Rescue unit, said he and his partner, Bert Randolph, 42, were searching the main hiking path when a dog barked.

"We investigated and here was this beautiful collie lying down next to the child. Laura was sleeping, her head on the collie," said Hoover. "It was incredible."

After the rescuers picked up the child, the dog trotted away into the night. "We didn't think much about it," said Hoover. "We were busy with Laura, checking her vital signs and making sure she wasn't hurt."

No one else saw the dog. Laura later said that there had been three dogs, but the collie had chased away the other two dogs. Rescuers said the other two "dogs" were probably coyotes who have become increasingly bold in the last few years, sometimes even roaming into urban neighborhoods.

The child was examined at the County General Hospital and let go. She was treated for minor scratches and abrasions.

Paramedics said that Laura would have gone into hypothermia as the temperatures were down in the lower forties last night. They attribute Laura's good health to the stray collie who kept her warm.

❧

Lassie, it had to be Lassie. Jimmy just knew it. He looked at the map and carefully highlighted the regional park where the girl was found. She was closer to home but still about seventy-five miles away. He carefully tore out the story, folded it, and tucked it into his wallet. He told himself his parents wouldn't care or wouldn't believe that the dog who had helped the little girl was Lassie. After all they were nearly home. They wouldn't turn back around, would they?

❧

"Who's your friend, Taber?" asked a thin brown man of about fifty. His grey-green eyes sparkled. His name was Luis and he came from Spain. He had been with the circus since he was a little boy because his parents were circus people, too. It was a family tradition. He and Taber were a team, and they had been together for many years now. No one seem to remember how this crazy chimpanzee came to join the circus, but over the years many acts had come and gone, and Taber had survived it all. The circus had become his home. Luis had befriended him and they had been together ever since.

Luis took Taber's outstretched hand and held it. "Ready for the show tonight, Taber?"

Taber nodded and hooted. Lassie jumped at the hoots, but didn't take her eyes off Taber.

"And who are you?" asked Luis to the dog. She politely sniffed his hand and allowed the man to stroke her head. Luis unbolted Taber's cage door and the chimp hopped down. He stood as tall as Lassie. That seemed to amuse Taber and he hooted again and patted Lassie's head and made smacking noises.

"Come on, Taber," said Luis. "I bet this chiquita is hungry." Taber took Luis's hand and with Lassie beside them they walked to a motor home parked behind an open tent lined with horses standing in straw. Next to the horses were the huge leathery animals. Elephants.

Luis opened the door of the mobile home and Taber hopped inside. "Come on, chiquita," said Luis kindly. "Are you hungry?"

That did it. Lassie knew the words meant food so she climbed up the three steps and walked inside the tiny house with the man and the chimpanzee. The door shut behind them.

❧

Home. The Harmons were home. But it wasn't home. Not anymore. It was cold and uninviting. No Lassie to greet them with her feathery white tail wagging and her happy barking. Her excitement was infectious. She seemed to fill the house with warmth and happiness.

Their house was dark inside. The porch light had burned out and the neighbors hadn't turned lights on tonight. Slowly they filed inside. Mom walked over to the neighbor's to pick up Sarah. Dad sorted through mail put on the kitchen table by neighbors, then he listened to the phone messages. Nothing about Lassie. Jimmy went upstairs and shut his bedroom door to prepare his plan. He'd find Lassie himself. He didn't need anyone else's help. He worked in his room until nine-thirty, yelled good-night to his parents and went to bed.

At one a.m. his alarm clock rang under his pillow. Instantly he woke and slammed it quiet. He made himself sit up so he wouldn't yield to temptation and curl up and go back to sleep.

Quietly, he pulled on the clothes he'd stashed under his bed. Black jeans. Black turtleneck. The dark blue cable sweater Grandma had knitted. His ski mask, gloves, hat, and heavy overcoat. Ninja dog hunter. In his backpack were the supplies he had packed that evening, a tightly rolled blanket, cans of dog food, a change of clothes, and the map.

Jimmy crept downstairs, eased open the kitchen door to the garage and slipped out to get his bike. As he opened the outside double door, the garage light flared on.

Dad stood in the kitchen doorway.

16

Meeting New Friends

Lassie spent the night with Luis and Taber in the trailer. He fed her and left her in his trailer to rest while he and Taber and the others in the circus put on their show. This was their first night in Waterloo and they didn't need any new distractions. Luis was the main clown and Taber was his sidekick. Much of the time they had had a dog or two working with them in the act. But his last dog had gotten too old to perform and Luis had given him to some friends to live out his old age. Maybe this bonita collie would fill in the empty place in his act and heart. She appeared young and smart. She and Taber were getting along, which was important. Some dogs hated the chimp. One never knew for sure how animals would respond to each other.

Taber rode a fat bellied pony named Mr. Chips into the ring. He was dressed as a cowboy, with hat, gun belt, pistols, chaps, and little red vest. Children loved Taber and he loved to be loved by them. He was so hooked on the attention from the audience that often he would throw a few added surprises into the act for extra applause.

Before and after his performance, Luis considered various possible acts with the collie. Perhaps Taber could be the owner, walking his dog. The collie could spy a pretend cat and chase after it, dragging Taber. Taber could fall. No, better he could fall onto a skateboard and the dog could race around dragging Taber after him.

Luis loved thinking up new acts. Some circuses used the same acts over and over again, but Luis got bored if he didn't shift things around, attempting new tricks. His animals seemed to like the changes, too.

Sometimes Mr. Chips, the fat pony, would refuse to obey Luis's cues and do something entirely different during an act. Most of the time it was a good change, too. Luis was glad his animals were creative and felt free enough to try new things without fear. Some trainers would beat an animal that didn't follow an act precisely. Luis wasn't that way.

Late that night Luis, Taber, and Lassie sat on Luis's bed. Luis was holding bits of glittery material up to Lassie, measuring, fitting her for a possible costume. Earlier he'd given her a bath and brushed her tattered fur.

She was a handsome dog. He was surprised she was running around loose with no collar. Someone must not have known or cared what a wonderful animal they'd had.

Taber carefully parted Lassie's fur with his clever fingers, grooming her monkey style.

Luis grinned. "You think she got bugs?" he asked the chimp. But Taber didn't find any bugs after running long fingers through her fur.

Tomorrow morning the three of them would have some free time and Luis would see how Lassie did in taking cues during an act.

✤

"Going somewhere?" Dad asked, his hand on the light switch.

"Someone has to do something!" Jimmy exploded. "You and mom are all happy to just forget about her!" He knew that wasn't completely true, but with the embarrassment of the moment, he couldn't seem to control his emotions.

"That's not true, son. But we have to be realistic."

"What does that mean? Realistic? That Lassie's gone forever?"

Dad looked pained. "I hope not. But someone may have found her and decided to keep her. It's hard to tell."

Jimmy suddenly was exhausted. The thought of riding his bike out into the cold night, pedaling for hours and hours seemed outrageous. The last sighting had been over seventy miles away. If that had been Lassie.

Besides, what did he think he'd do for food for example? Steal food? He could imagine getting arrested and hauled off to jail. "But officers, I'm just trying to find my dog." They'd be real sympathetic especially when they found out he was a preacher's kid. Oh, just another wild PK.

"I don't know what to do," Jimmy blurted out and unexpectedly he began to cry, like a big, blubbering baby. He hated himself for crying, but he couldn't stop.

Dad crossed the garage floor and took him in his arms. "It's OK to cry," Dad said as he held Jimmy close. A million moments of worry and anxiety seemed to wash away as Jimmy stood there holding his dad.

❧

Luis walked around a practice ring with Lassie heeling off leash. She followed him right, left, slow, fast, precisely. "Someone has spent some time training you," he said to the dog. "You're a fine dog." When they finished, Luis showed Lassie the other animals in the circus.

At first, she didn't want to come close to the elephants, but Luis coaxed her.

"This is Mariah," said Luis to Lassie. "She's the oldest elephant here, an Asian elephant. She's thirty-four years old. She's very wise."

Mariah uncurled her trunk and reached it out towards Lassie. The dog leaned against Luis's leg and whined. He patted Lassie, then stroked Mariah's trunk. "That's right, Mariah, say hello to this bonita chiquita."

Lassie sniffed the hay scent of the elephant. Its clear brown eyes examined Lassie calmly and Lassie relaxed,

108

sensing a gentleness in the huge creature.

"Bueno," said Luis. "You are worthy of each other. Intelligent, you both are." Lassie could tell the elephant was also a friend of man, a protector and helper.

Luis gave Mariah a handful of grain and then he and Lassie moved on, past the four other Asian elephants shifting in the straw, their high legs bound by heavy chains. But not Mariah. She was trustworthy and sensible. She would never run away or do damage. In fact, it was Mariah who helped haul some of the heavy poles from the tents during the many set ups and tear downs of the circus. She was better than a forklift because she could think about what she was doing.

Ten palomino horses stood near the elephants, also bedded in straw. They were tied with halters and ropes to a picket line. Two ponies, one was Mr. Chips, were on the far side of the horses. Both ponies were fat bellied, sweet tempered, and the color of chocolate chip ice cream—thick with chips. The ponies nickered a welcome. They belonged to Luis and he treated them like he did all his animals, as if they were his children.

He fed the ponies grain from his hand and petted their bushy white manes. Lassie wasn't the least bit afraid of horses or ponies and Luis was pleased by what he sensed in Lassie.

"Now for the tigers," he said. He and Lassie walked out

of the tent to a row of individual cages that held the tigers.

Lassie didn't like the tigers. She smelled their scent even before she entered the circus grounds. They made her uneasy. They reminded her of mountain lions, only more arrogant. Two of the seven tigers were white with cream-colored stripes instead of the normal black and orange stripes.

Luis noticed Lassie shivered and he patted her. "It's okay. They make me scared, too." He ruled out using a tiger in his act with Lassie. He didn't mind. Working with tigers was always tricky at best. A trainer never had the big cats' confidence or trust as he had with horses, dogs, chimps, or elephants.

"What do you think about making a debut tonight, my pretty girl?" asked Luis. "Do you think you could handle it?"

Lassie was just glad to be walking away from the golden eyes of the tigers and gave a happy bark.

Luis was delighted at her response. "It's settled then. Let's do a couple run throughs, and you'll be my newest star."

17

A Star Is Born

"**W**ould you really run away?" Katie asked Jimmy during lunch at school several days later.

"I wasn't running away," he said quietly. "I was going to look for Lassie."

Tears crowded Katie's eyes. "I feel so bad," she began.

Jimmy stood up, his brown bag lunch unopened. "I don't want to talk about it," he said and walked off. Tears ran down Katie's cheeks.

"What's the matter?" asked an older girl nastily. "Boyfriend dump you?"

Katie ignored the girl, picked up her lunch and Jimmy's and threw them both in the trash. Katie retreated to the library and did homework and didn't see Jimmy again that day.

❧

Luis was delighted with Lassie. He devised a simple part for her in the act. Taber walked her on a leash. He was dressed like a proper gentleman, little three piece suit with a top hat. As they completed a walk in the front of the arena, Luis dressed in a big fuzzy cat costume jumped out. Lassie bolted after him. Luis started running. Taber jumped onto a skateboard, still holding the leash attached to Lassie's harness.

She pulled him for a wild ride twice around the ring. The second time around Taber pulled on a string tied to a little pack on Lassie's glittery harness. Out popped a small parachute, which supposedly slowed Lassie.

The crowd loved it. Luis could tell by the way Taber eagerly got into place to begin his act that he liked working with a dog again. Luis enjoyed working with a dog again, too. It seemed to Luis that Lassie had fun being in front of an audience.

"A natural ham," said one of the circus girls named Anna. She had emigrated from Poland with her father, mother, and brother, who were in the tightrope act. Anna and her father worked the palomino horses and she danced on their backs.

"Maybe I can borrow your dog?" asked Anna with a heavy accent. "She matches my horses, no?" The tawny part of Lassie's color did match the gold of Anna's horses.

Luis shook his head no, grinned back and teased, "She's too valuable to waste on those horses."

"Oh, plee-uuze," drawled Anna and put her arms around Lassie. "You are loveliness," she whispered to the dog.

The circus was in Waterloo for ten days. Even though it had been fun and exciting, there was a loneliness in Lassie's heart that the circus could not fill. Luis fed and took care of her, but she needed to continue her journey. But how? How could she get away?

On the eleventh day, Lassie sensed something in the air. The atmosphere was different from other days. Everyone started packing up and getting ready to move on to a special benefit performance in Dubuque for a children's hospital. Dubuque was only a few miles from the Harmons home.

❧

A couple weeks after Lassie had vanished, Jimmy, Katie, and Rags walked behind the hardware store. The BMX'ers spun around their track, jumping off ramps and over ditches filled with mucky water.

"Hey," said one kid, skidding beside them. "Heard anything about your dog?"

Jimmy shook his head. "Nothing more." He was tired of being asked the same old question and never having an answer. He had continued running the ad in the paper. A couple people called, but the dogs weren't Lassie. One turned out to be a poodle-mix. He couldn't believe it. Some people didn't even know the difference! He guessed for reward money people would try anything.

"Sorry, man," said the kid. "We're still praying. Not around the clock. Kind of hard to wake up at night for too long, you know? But we're praying."

"Thanks," said Jimmy. He really appreciated those kids, but his hope was gone. It had drained away the night Dad found him ready to leave to look for Lassie on his own.

Jimmy was mad at his parents. At God, too. Why wouldn't his parents help look more for Lassie? And why wouldn't God answer his prayer and send Lassie home?

He could understand that maybe Lassie had been taken away to help people, the way he was sure she'd helped that little girl who was lost in the park. And the way she'd helped keep Maggie's horse under control. Though Jimmy wondered why God didn't use some other dog. Why Lassie?

A little voice said, Why not Lassie? Isn't she God's dog after all? He gave her to you.

God's dog, huh? Okay, fine, God, he thought. *You take care of her then. I'm not going to worry anymore. I'm going to forget she ever existed.*

And he did.

At least he pretended to. He never talked about her anymore. He tried to get out of any conversation about her. He forbade Katie to bring up the subject.

But at night. Ha! That was totally different. His dreams were engulfed with Lassie. Lassie, Lassie, Lassie. Real happenings. Old memories dredged up. Stuff he'd forgotten. Then made-up scenarios. Some were so happy and pleasant that he didn't want to wake up. But some awful, nightmares. Lassie got mad, foaming at the mouth, snapping, biting, eyes red rimmed, a monster dog, a cyber canine.

Some dreams were bizarre. Lassie talking to him. Telling him what a lousy master he was. Lassie preaching at church telling everyone there was no God. That was about the worst. Bone chilling, stomach sickening.

Lassie. Lassie. Lassie.

He just couldn't deal with the dreams, with her, with any of it anymore. He just wanted to forget all about her. If only he could.

The kids praying were being great, but he just couldn't deal with it. "I gotta go home," said Jimmy.

Katie gave him a funny look. "You just got here."

He tried to smile. "I know, but I forgot I have to do something." Did that sound lame or what? He didn't look at Katie again because if he did he might not be able to leave. He knew she would have an incredibly hurt look on her face. He jogged away.

⚓

The last show before they travelled to the charity show at Dubuque, Lassie invented a new ending for her act.

After she raced twice around the ring with Taber madly hanging ten on the skateboard, they completed their normal routine of Lassie's parachute bursting open, Taber letting go of her leash, and Taber and Lassie returning to Luis. But instead of running off stage, Lassie detoured, jumped over the low wall to the bleachers and visited the first row full of children from the local YMCA.

For several minutes, Lassie went from child to child, nuzzling shy children, allowing them to stroke her, finger her sparkling harness, lift the light parachute. Finally, when the palomino horses began to file in, Luis, with Taber sitting on his hip like a child, his long hairy arms around his master's neck, whistled softly and said, "Heel, chiquita."

Lassie gave a final swipe of the tongue to a child and ran to Luis. When they left the ring, the sound of clapping drowned out the pounding of forty galloping hooves tattooing the sawdust floor.

18

A Needed Diversion

"I'm not going," Jimmy protested. He sat in his room in the middle of his bed with the new Road and Track magazine spread out on his lap. "And you can't make me," Jimmy added.

Dad leaned against the door jam, arms folded over his chest. "Jimmy you can't hide for the rest of your life."

Oh, yes, I can, he thought. You, on the other hand, are just bugged because you can't get me to do what you want. Your obedient little Christian son is rebelling. God forbid, what will the church people think, huh? Your precious reputation might suffer, huh?

Be cool, he warned himself. Be cool. "I'm not hiding, Dad. I just don't want to go to the circus, okay? That's for little kids. I'm not interested. Thank you for thinking of me." This wasn't the reasonable Jesus-as-a-kid in the temple, but a mutated, icy version that Jimmy was perfecting, if he did say so himself.

Dad finally gave up trying to convince him. When he

left, Jimmy hopped up and shut his bedroom door. He glanced at the clock. Good, they'd be leaving for church to get the youth group in about ten minutes and they'd be gone for a couple hours. He'd have some peace and quiet.

In the past, his parents were usually pretty good, he hadn't had any major complaints, but now they would not leave him alone. "Jimmy, come with me to the store." "Jimmy, come watch television with us." "Jimmy, you're always alone. Call Katie or someone else to come over."

Blah, blah, blah. They chattered at him like demented blue jays. He was sick of it. He wished he had the nerve to go hunt for Lassie again. But he didn't. He was too chicken to try sneaking out again.

Three weeks had passed since she was gone and it was as if she had dropped off the face of the earth. After that story about Lassie finding the little kid, he didn't hear or see anything about her. No one called anymore about the classified ad, even about the wrong dog. What more could he do? He wanted go back up to the area she was last seen this weekend and leave more flyers but his parents said, No, they were supposed to take the youth group to the circus.

Get a life. As if the youth group couldn't go to the circus without them. Besides Mom didn't have to go. She could have driven him up there to look for Lassie.

So he wouldn't betray Lassie and go have fun while his dog was missing? His parents better think again.

He threw his magazine across the room and laid back on his bed. He just wanted to sleep.

The doorbell rang downstairs. He ignored it. It rang again. Go away, he told whoever was out there. But instead the front door opened.

Great, his father probably was back to work on him again. He jumped up about to run into the bathroom when Katie called up the stairs. "Jimmy?"

❦

Luis was brushing Lassie's long fur carefully. "Okay, chiquita, let's get you and Taber dressed." Luis buttoned the jacket and Taber hooted. "I know, you love to perform, no?"

Then turning to Lassie, Luis slipped on her sequined harness and checked the parachute to be sure it was packed properly and would pull out straight.

Luis had already groomed Mr. Chips. The pony had been combed so a checkerboard pattern decorated his rump. Metallic ribbons were braided in his mane and tail and he wore a child's western saddle and sparkling bridle for his act with the cowboy chimp.

Luis dressed himself last. A clown's outfit for now. He'd throw on the cat costume later. His wild pink hair like a plastic troll's, stood straight up. Baggy suit, oversized black shoes. He carefully made up his face. White grease paint. Big wide red smile. Triangles of blue over his eyebrows.

Rubber red nose. He put on his white gloves and they were ready!

🔱

"You have to come to the circus, now!" screamed Katie. She stood at the foot of the stairs. Jimmy stared down at her. He'd never heard her scream like that before.

She stamped her foot. "I'm sick of you acting like this. Someone would think you'd never had a disappointment before. Well, I'm telling you to get used to it. Life isn't fair, Jimmy. Figure it out!"

His breath rasped in his throat. He couldn't answer her.

She marched upstairs and into his room. She threw open his closet door, snatched his jacket, came back out and threw it at him. Automatically he caught his jacket.

"Let's go, now," she commanded and took his arm.

He had no choice. He followed her outside and got into her father's truck, squeezing between Katie and her little brother, Max.

They met up with the youth group outside the ticket booth. Scents of straw, popcorn, hotdogs and warm animals curled around them.

If his parents were surprised to see him, they didn't show it. He was glad for that. No one else acted surprised to see him, so he was relieved not to deal with that.

Twenty-five youth group members squeezed in among other rows of kids. Katie, Jimmy, and some of the older kids sat about half way up the bleachers to let the younger kids get up close so they could see.

It had been a long time since he'd seen a circus. He thought a moment. *It must have been when I was seven. Before Lass—*

He stopped himself, never realizing how his life had been neatly divided into two categories, before Lassie and Lassie in the family. Now there was an after Lassie category. He wanted to cry, right then and there, but, of course, he didn't.

Forget about it, he told himself. *It's over, remember? She's gone. Don't think about her. Just concentrate on now. Have fun.* Yeah, right. He didn't think he'd ever have fun again. So he said to himself, *At least pretend to have fun. Don't ruin everybody else's' fun.* He sighed heavily. He would try for their sakes, . . . really try.

He turned to Katie. "I'm glad you talked me into coming," he said with a fake smile.

She stared at him as if he was sprouting a second head. She put her hand on his forehead. "Do you have a fever?"

Just then the houselights dropped and the ringmaster stepped into a brilliant pool of light.

"Welcome to the finest circus on earth!" he boomed.

19

The Cool White Tiger

As the elephants trod over to the big top, Lassie sat with Taber as Luis bridled Mr. Chips. The pony chewed on his bit and stomped an impatient forefoot.

"Steady old man," said Luis, chuckling and slapping the pony's shoulder.

"Full house tonight," said Anna as she passed by on her way to get the horses for her act.

"Usually is for a charity," said Luis.

"I'm a little nervous," admitted Anna. "We're using that new tiger tonight. He's kind of well, unruly, I think. But you know Papa. He wants to use the white tiger."

Luis nodded. "Your Papa is a good trainer. All will go well, you'll see."

Anna bit her lip as she untied five of the horses, all wearing red plumes on top of their bridles.

"That tiger, Papa calls him Andrej. He swiped at one of my horses yesterday during practice. Look, part of Lucia's tail is missing."

Luis looked. Sure enough. The creamy tail swept over the horse's hocks. One side looked as if someone chopped it off with giant scissors.

"I'm not sure who was madder—Lucia or me!" said Anna. "I'm taking a bull whip with me tonight. I don't trust Andrej."

Luis watched Anna lead the five horses out, three in one hand, two in the other. The horses were lovely, the color of gold satin. Their beauty was enhanced when they performed all by themselves without any help from Anna. If they didn't want to obey, they could leave. But the horses never did.

The grand finale of their act was when three tigers who did not have any physical restraints entered the ring to perform with the horses.

The tigers silked out, two tawny and jungle-striped, the other the icy cool white tiger, Andrej. The crowd gasped as the feline forms rippled out to the center of the ring. They sprang onto the bright colored wooden boxes as the trotting horses tightened their circle around them.

Luis led his troupe to the proper entrance and waited in the cool night air. Lassie whined softly, her ears pricked intently as she heard the roar of the tigers. Luis knew she didn't like the tigers, but unless she was near them, she had learned to ignore them, as all the animals did. None of the animals liked being near the tigers, especially Andrej.

As a matter of fact, most of the people didn't either.

Two horses cantered around the ring as the other three halted, one beside each tiger, standing with tails arched, heads high, plumes dancing.

Anna's father cracked his whip. One tiger sprang from his stool and galloped the opposite direction of the running horses. Then the tawny tiger jumped into the air, sailing over the back of the first standing horse. As the tiger hit the other side, the horse bolted as if shot out of a gun and joined the other two horses in running around the ring.

The whip cracked a second time. The other orange tiger sprang down into the ring, leaving cool looking Andrej snarling on his stool. As Luis watched from the entrance, Lassie's whine turned into a growl.

"Hush, chiquita," he murmured. "Hush. It's all right."

The second tiger cut in and sprang over another standing horse. Then that horse spun off under the lights to join his pals and the other tawny tiger loped along behind his brother.

The whip cracked a third time, but Andrej didn't jump down.

Jimmy leaned forward, elbows on his knees watching the pale tiger. He wasn't sure if the cat's rebellion was part of the act or not. It looked like it wasn't, but then that's what they wanted you to think. Sort of like the highwire artist falling from the wire. They did it on purpose to make it look like they lost their balance and fell.

The whip cracked closer to the tiger's face. The trainer shouted. The big cat only snarled. Even from where Jimmy was sitting, he could see the animal's long fangs. Its lightly striped tail lashed back and forth, slicing the air. The horse that Andrej was supposed to jump over was trembling, sweat breaking out on its shoulders. It tossed its head so its mane shimmered like beaten silver.

"Gosh," breathed Katie. "That tiger is scary."

Jimmy had to agree with her. It looked scary at least. He whispered back trying to sound cool, "It's just the act." But he wasn't so sure.

Finally after two more whip cracks, the tiger hopped down and circled the horse. It didn't run around the ring like the other tigers continued to do, but merely faced the trainer and snarled. Suddenly the standing horse broke and spurted past the tiger to run with the others. *Safety in numbers,* thought Jimmy, and didn't blame the horse at all.

Crack! The whip snapped. Suddenly, the tiger leaped at the trainer.

The audience gasped. Women began to scream. Jimmy wanted to hold his hands over his ears, but instead he gripped the arm rests of his seat and wouldn't let go.

The tremendous strength of the tiger's paw caused Anna's father to reel back, stumble against a wooden block, and fall down. Anna didn't waste time screaming, but quickly took up her bull whip and gave it a powerful crack. The lash struck the cat across its back. The tiger roared and ran a few paces; then stopped and turned back, lips curled in a snarl. Anna's father pulled himself up, holding his side. The tiger flattened its ears and began to stalk the man. Stealthily, it moved closer, closer, closer. The tiger may be declawed, but he still had teeth.

From the side of the big tent a blur of caramel colored fur sprang into the ring, darting behind the tiger. She raked the tiger's haunch with her teeth. The big cat turned unbelievably fast, doubling over itself. But if Lassie was surprised she didn't falter. She barked, teasing the tiger to follow her, follow her away from the hurt trainer.

When Lassie barked, Jimmy sat bolt upright, his hands gripping the arm rests of the bleachers even harder. His knuckles turned white. His nails dug into the cheap wood of the arm rests. His brain shouted, *That's Lassie! It's her bark!*

20

The Best Night of All

Katie turned to Jimmy, her eyes wide, startled, at his transformation. She quickly put her hand on his rigid arm. "No, it can't be, Jimmy. That can't be Lassie."

Quickly, Jimmy shot a glance down the row of seats to where his dad sat. But his dad was on his feet in frozen disbelief. Jimmy knew that his dad had recognized the bark, too. At that moment, they were both thinking the same thing.

His gaze returned to the dog who was drawing the tiger backwards, step by step, alternating between teasing with barks and switching to dart behind the tiger to drive the cat forward.

Anna helped her father gain his foothold and assisted him in getting out of the ring. Assistant trainers caught the scared horses and led them away.

The white tiger's crate sat empty, waiting for the terrible dance to the end. Finally, the cat snarled in defeat and bolted into his crate. A handler slammed the door shut.

The audience relaxed and nearly everyone let out a sigh of relief.

Jimmy flexed his fingers and sighed. "I guess you're right," he whispered to Katie. "It couldn't be Lassie." Just another collie who looked kind of like her. Another collie who acted like her. Sounded like her. It couldn't possibly be Lassie.

His heart pounded as if he'd just sprinted to the end of a two mile race.

He glanced again at his dad, but Mr. Harmon was now seated and out of his view.

With the ring darkened, the ringmaster in his circle of light tried to soothe the crowd with words about how training tigers was dangerous business, but the trainer would be fine, just had a few bruised ribs. They had thought the new tiger was ready to be worked, but they had misjudged his readiness. When he mentioned the tiger's name was Ferocity, the crowd laughed nervously.

In minutes the ring was cleared and ready for the next act.

The clowns trooped in.

Jimmy laughed automatically as clowns capered and performed magic tricks. Then a chimpanzee dressed like a business man came out strolling along with the collie who'd tamed the tiger. Jimmy sat up straighter unaware of the worried glance of Katie on him. He focused his whole being on the collie.

When Lassie appeared, the crowd burst into appreciative applause for the dog who tamed the angry tiger. Jimmy didn't clap, but sat like a marble statue, his eyes gazed hungrily on the dog. Oh, how the dog looked like Lassie. His whole body ached like he had the flu. He wondered if perhaps he should excuse himself and go to the restroom. Why was he putting himself through this kind of agony? No one would blame him if he couldn't watch a dog just like Lassie. He stood up.

Katie gave him a questioning look.

"Gotta go to the bathroom," he muttered and squeezed past many knees to the aisle.

Katie started to get up after him, but when Jimmy froze standing on the aisle steps, she waited.

Lassie and Taber went through their act with Jimmy watching from the aisle. Lassie charged after the clown dressed up as a house cat. Taber acted wildly out of control, flying behind Lassie on the skateboard. Then the parachute popped out and slowed her down. The audience loved it. As Luis and Taber took bows, Lassie began to visit the children in the first row.

More applause greeted the beautiful collie as she nuzzled the eager children. Like in a dream, Jimmy began walking down the steps.

"Jimmy," called Katie, scrambling after him, tripping over feet.

"Jimmy, Jimmy," called Mr. Harmon to no avail from his seat. Jimmy didn't even turn his head. He was beyond hearing.

Jimmy descended the steps and stopped at the first row. He tried to snap his fingers and whistle to the dog, but his fingers were stiff and his mouth was so dry that no sound came out.

Slowly Lassie worked down the row greeting kids. She suddenly lifted her head, her liquid eyes widening. She sucked in more air.

That scent! That beloved scent!

At that moment, Jimmy and Lassie locked gazes. Immediately they recognized each other.

That face! That beloved face!

Luis was standing nearby watching, puzzled when Lassie didn't return when he whistled for her. He saw the boy gawking at the dog. Then all of a sudden he understood and smiled.

Lassie gave a single yelp and flung herself at Jimmy. He threw wide his arms as the collie bulleted into him, knocking him down on the steps. People around them stared, then began laughing, as if unsure if this was part of the act or not. The crowd went wild with applause. This was truly the greatest show on earth.

Luis walked over and put a hand on Lassie's head. "I see you two have met before," he said with a grin.

All Jimmy could do was grin. He had no words to say at that moment. All he wanted to do was hug Lassie.

By this time, Mr. and Mrs, Harmon, Sarah, Katie, and half of their youth group were down in the front wanting to pet Lassie. Mr. Harmon told all the kids to return to their seats for the rest of the show.

"Why don't we go outside and have a little talk." Luis motioned to Jimmy to follow him out of the nearest exit. Then Jimmy and his dad, Lassie, and Luis walked away together. The thunderous sounds of applause followed them out the door.

Jimmy couldn't remember a night more special than this one.

21

New Horizons

Jimmy, Lassie, Katie, and Rags walked along the BMX™ track behind Madison's Hardware store. The boys on their bikes had slowed down and pedaled over to greet Lassie. They petted and praised her for her tiger taming performance. The news had spread like wildfire. The story had been in all the papers. Jimmy thanked them again for their prayers—it seemed they were the faithful ones!

"Hey, guys" Jimmy said when things had calmed down a little. "I want to thank you again for praying for Lassie . . . and for me. It really cheered me up when we were searching to know that someone was praying for us."

"No problem, Jimmy," the oldest biker responded. "It helped us, too."

The bikers rode off to the track and the two friends walked through the spring grass, kicking small mushrooms while the canines chased each other.

Jimmy put his hands in his jacket pockets, smiling as Lassie whirled around to tease Rags with a bark. How fast she'd been when taunting that tiger. Brave, too. As brave as Daniel in the lions' den. Braver than he, Jimmy, had been, that was for sure. He could learn a lot from his dog.

Luis, the man who'd been taking care of Lassie, told him how Lassie had come to join the circus. Luis hadn't read the classified ads, he only had time to scan headlines, and besides his English reading wasn't as good as his Spanish. He apologized to Jimmy.

"I see so many animals that people dump, it just didn't occur to me to check," he said. "But Someone has been watching over Lassie, that's for sure," he added after Jimmy told him some of the adventures Lassie had been involved since her fateful truck ride. Who knew what else she had done? Only Lassie and God.

Later after the tiger taming act, his parents had met with Luis and he had told them, "Any time Jimmy wants a job training animals, send him to me. He did a good job training this dog. He'd be a good circus worker." Jimmy liked that. Maybe he would train other animals when he got older.

Then Luis had given Jimmy his business card with the circus's business address on it. "I'm serious," Luis told him and patted Jimmy's shoulder. Then he'd stroked Lassie's head and whispered something in Spanish to her. Jimmy was curious what Luis had said, but didn't think it was polite to ask.

At home, Jimmy tucked the business card carefully

away along with the two newspaper stories and a classified ad clipping about Lassie.

One thing was certain, Someone *did* watch over Lassie. Someone *did* keep her safe, even when Jimmy was not able to put into words how he felt. There was comfort in knowing that, but he was sure God would put him to the test another time.

For now, things could get back to normal. Well, almost. After all, what was normal when you figured God, Jimmy, and Lassie into the equation?

Treasure at Eagle Mountain

"Did you say there is treasure in these woods?"

Camping is by far Jimmy Harmon's most favorite thing to do. He and his dad and Uncle Cully have been making plans for months. Every time Jimmy takes something out of the closet, Lassie gets excited. She can't wait, either.

Little do they know that an abandoned shack, a mysterious inscription, a hidden treasure, and a pair of dark eyes staring at them through the trees will provide an adventure they will not soon forget.

"Sometimes the best and worst in a man comes out when he is out in the woods," Paul Harmon tells his son. Jimmy wasn't sure what that means but he is confident that God will be with them no matter what happens.

Chariot Books®
*A Division of Cook
Communications Ministries*

To the Rescue

"Everybody needs help. God uses us to help 'em."

That's what Mr. Krebs needs all right—help! Ever since Jimmy Harmon volunteered to mastermind a project to find homes for the stray animals from the animal shelter, he's felt good about himself. He is finally going to make a difference *all on his own.* He makes posters, puts signs in stores, calls his friends to help groom and display the animals, the whole works. Everything is working smoothly . . . until Mr. Krebs calls the animal control people.

Mr. Krebs thinks the shelter animals are mangy, dirty, and dangerous, . . . and should be put to sleep. How could anyone feel that way about animals? Jimmy isn't even sure God can change his neighbor's mind. But Lassie and some orphaned puppies teach Mr. Krebs a lesson, and at the same time help Jimmy realize that no one is beyond hope and out of God's reach.

Chariot Books
*A Division of Cook
Communications Ministries*